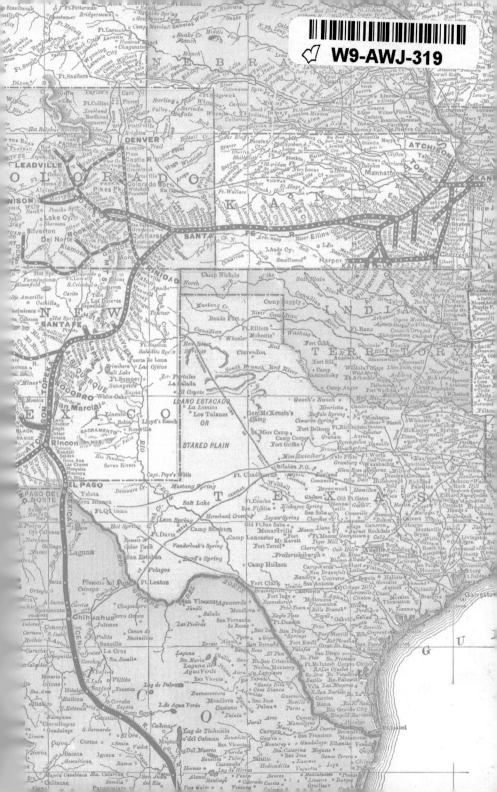

When Molly Was a Harvey Girl

When Molly Was a
Harvey Girl

By Frances M. Wood

Kane Miller
A DIVISION OF EDC PUBLISHING

First Edition 2010
Kane Miller, A Division of EDC Publishing

Copyright © Frances M. Wood, 2010

For information contact:
Kane Miller, A Division of EDC Publishing
PO Box 470663
Tulsa, OK 74147-0663
www.kanemiller.com
www.edcpub.com

Library of Congress Control Number: 2009934750

Cover design: Kat Godard, DraDog, LLC

Manufactured by Regent Publishing Services, Hong Kong
Printed May 2010 in ShenZhen, Guangdong, China
1 2 3 4 5 6 7 8 9 10

ISBN: 978-1-935279-51-8

✦ ✦ ✦

With great love I dedicate this book to that Colorado photographer extraordinaire — Ed Wood, Jr. — who just happens to be the great-grandson of a Harvey Girl.

And special thanks go to:
the wonderful writers of WINCbooks.com,
especially Louise Hawes, Jackie Ogburn, and Billie Hurmence;
and Jennifer Weltz of the Jean V. Naggar Literary Agency,
who kept faith that *Molly* would grow up to be a *real* book.

Chapter 1

"Corn is the life-sustenance of Illinois." *The Atchison, Topeka and Santa Fe Railway Guidebook*

By late summer, Molly could always smell the corn growing. And when the day was hot and humid, as it was today, the smell was so strong she could almost eat corn out of the air. So it was corn that she smelled and tasted when she closed her eyes, while she waited for Jonathan to kiss her.

Jonathan's forehead bumped against hers. Now Molly smelled a pleasant kind of boy sweat, and the odor of homemade soap. Their noses touched. Molly pursed her lips.

"K-I-S-S-I-N-G!"

Jonathan's chin knocked Molly's in his hurry to get away.

Her first kiss, ruined!

There they were, the rest of the seventh grade class – all six of them. Like Molly and Jonathan, they had snuck away from the school's summer picnic. Molly and Jonathan's path must have been obvious – broken leaves and bent stalks through the wind-waving corn. Now the people who were supposed to be their friends mocked with eyes half-closed, lips pursed. Wilson clasped his hands tightly against his chest, as if languishing for love.

Jonathan blushed. His tanned skin took on a red tone, like mahogany wood. Molly's belly burned with anger. Her fury volcanoed upward – and then erupted as helpless, sputtering laughter. "You!" she accused Amy. This was such a typical Amy joke.

Amy laughed back, pleased with herself.

Wilson rolled his eyes. "Oh, Romeo," he falsettoed. "Oh, Juliet," his voice dropped to a deep bass.

"Oh, *please*!" Molly could hardly get the words out.

Jonathan couldn't speak at all. He backed away. "Going home," he finally managed, his words as embarrassed as his face. "Help Pa with that broken axle."

Wilson took pity on his friend. "I'll come." The other boys followed. They ran away, shouting boasts and dares, chasing each other down the cornstalk aisles.

Amy waited until they were gone, then demanded, "How many times did he kiss you?"

The other girls waited.

Molly could have answered honestly – or not. But she decided to be mysterious, to let the girls think whatever they wanted. Which, of course, would be so much more than what had actually happened. She flounced out of the cornfield and onto the road. Amy caught up with her. "Did you kiss him back?"

Molly was prim. "Thank you so much for letting me stay over at your home last night," she said, right out of an etiquette book. "It was ever so convenient, getting to the picnic early."

"Oh, Molly," Amy begged, "tell me! Did he open his mouth?"

"Please thank your mother for her hospitality." Molly gave Amy a wicked grin.

"Molly!"

Tomorrow Molly would tell Amy everything … maybe. But for now, she danced down the road, leaving Amy and the other girls howling with frustration and laughter behind her.

Cornfields and more cornfields. Molly passed Amy's farm, where she kept a nightgown folded in a drawer in Amy's bedroom. She slowed and then lingered in front of Jonathan's gate. The boys were probably inside the big tool shed behind the house. A year ago they had all been small and squeaky. Wilson still was. But now Jonathan's voice was deeper, and he was almost Molly's height. He was the most handsome boy in the seventh, soon to be eighth, grade. It was amazing how much a person could change in a year.

Molly let her eyelashes drift downward. No matter that she could scarcely see. Her feet knew this road well enough to travel it all on their own. She imagined: after the corn was harvested, after school started, after they were once again together every day, she would invite Jonathan to eat lunch with her behind the big oak tree. She would sit close beside him. She would put a piece of apple between his lips. She would watch him chew. She would move forward and inhale the scent of winesap. She would, just accidentally, touch her lips to his …

It would be so wonderful!

She imagined the kiss down to its smallest details: the soft whoosh of Jonathan's breath as their lips met; the swooning sensation that would begin in her throat and travel all the way down to her toes.

Her toes! Ow!

Molly's eyes popped open. She'd stubbed her toe on the paved beginning of Main Street. Somehow, during her excursion into romance, she had walked almost a mile. The hard-packed and rutted dirt had turned into brick pavement – and town.

"Molly!"

She continued to examine her toe. No blood.

"Molly Gerry!"

It was the proprietor of the livery stable who was calling out to her.

"Molly!" The candy store lady came rushing from her shop, arms open wide.

"Molly!" But it was the newspaper boy who got to Molly first. He thrust a copy of the weekly paper at her chest.

"Special Edition. August 20, 1890. Prominent Merchant Passes Today."

Papa.

That was how Molly found out. Papa was dead.

Yesterday, when she'd left town, he had been no different than last week, or last month – barely able to smile at her, hardly able to say her name. But alive. Colleen, Molly's older sister, had been matter-of-fact about Molly's plan to spend the night and day away. Colleen was always matter-of-fact. "Just say goodbye before you go," she told Molly.

So Molly kissed the dry, dull skin of Papa's cheek. "I'll tell you everything when I get home," she'd promised. And then she'd left, like she always left, with Colleen in charge.

Now, more than anything in the world, Molly wanted Colleen. But the good citizens of Streator, Illinois, kept stopping her. They wanted to murmur condolences, to pat her shoulder. They acted as if her feelings were something they could understand. The butcher even wept. The mayor's wife said what everybody was saying: "I'm so sorry."

Sorry?

What did these people know about sorrow? They hadn't spent the last year smelling alcohol, laudanum, brandy, blood – all the odors of unbearable illness. They hadn't come home from school to hear Papa's groans turn to moans, and those moans grow louder and more anguished as the months dragged on. They hadn't watched Colleen try to stroke the pain out of Papa's brow while the doctor prodded and pulled at Papa's disease-tormented body.

Molly unstuck herself from acquaintance after friend after acquaintance. Finally, she reached the blessed refuge of her own front door. But when she opened it, there were neighbors in the vestibule, the hall, the two parlors, the dining room – even the kitchen. They all wanted to hug Molly, to console themselves through consoling her.

She pushed through them toward the stairs. No arms would grab her there. Even next-door neighbors knew that upstairs was where a family was allowed to grieve in private.

She made it. She was almost up to the second floor landing. She was there. Down the hallway to the right was Papa's door, now closed. But the door to Papa's little dressing room stood open. That was where Colleen had slept for most of the past year.

Molly stopped just outside the dressing room door. Colleen sat on the narrow daybed, gazing out the window at the top of the maple tree as if she had never seen it before. She hadn't heard Molly's footsteps.

Molly went to stand in front of her sister. Colleen blinked, as if awakening. Then she smiled. Colleen wasn't a touching, hugging, clutching kind of person. But her smile gave Molly all the comfort she needed.

"I'm so glad, Molly," Colleen whispered. "I'm so happy for poor Papa."

I'm so happy for poor Papa. Molly held those words tight
in her mind during the days that followed. Colleen's words
were a truth that kept Molly going, through the funeral,
the wake, the everlasting visits from friends and neighbors.
Molly only had to be courteous and grateful. Colleen handled
everything else. Colleen was nineteen years old and as much
an adult as the doctor, the lawyer, or the priest. Colleen made
arrangements and signed papers. Molly only had to murmur,
"Thank you," and accept the gifts of cakes, pies, hams, roasts,
breads, and casseroles.

When the funeral week was over, she helped Colleen
wrap up the remaining food to give away to the poor. Molly
regretted this. The funeral food was the best they'd eaten since
their last cook quit sometime in the middle of Papa's illness.
But, "It will spoil, otherwise," Colleen said.

So Molly wrapped with brown butcher paper while
Colleen wrote out little thank-you notes on embossed
stationary. Each newly-clean dish would be returned with a
message. Colleen wrote and wrote. Molly finished wrapping.
With nothing else to do, she wandered into the vestibule.
For a whole week she had longed for silence, but now the big
house felt so empty. The cuckoo clock in the north parlor
chirped the hour. The great pendulum clock on the second
floor landing sent down an avalanche of bongs.

Molly ran upstairs, into the bongs. But too soon, the

pendulum clock quieted. Upstairs was as uncomfortably silent as downstairs. She went into her room to pull open her wardrobe door. It made a nice, homey, comforting click. She stared at her dresses. Six Mother Hubbards, once green, blue, pink, plaid, gingham, and patterned, now all dyed black. Now all exactly the same except for tiny details of sleeves or smocking.

How much time would have to pass before Molly could ask Colleen to sew mother-of-pearl buttons down the fronts? Or narrow pastel ribbons along the edges of the ruffles? Papa's favorite color had been green. How many months of mourning were required before Molly could wear green again?

"Molly?" Colleen was upstairs now too. She was calling from her room next door.

Molly went to look at herself in Colleen's big cheval mirror. Dressed in charcoal from hair bow to shoes, she appeared less a reflection than a shadow. Colleen was a shadow too, but in a tightly-waisted black gown with a fall of lace over her bosom and a bustle in the back. Colleen came to stand beside Molly so that the mirror reflected a picture of double mourning: two sisters of almost equal height, one a girl, the other a young lady.

"Good," Colleen said, apropos of nothing.

"I don't think so," Molly said.

Colleen left the mirror to go open a carved blanket chest. She removed a long, dove-gray dress with a velvet collar.

"Gray?" Molly exclaimed. "You're going to wear gray?"

And then she recognized the collar. "That was Mama's!"

Colleen held the gray bodice up against Molly's torso. Molly rubbed her cheek against the velvet, and almost remembered. "Did Mama wear rose perfume?"

"Roses of Loveliness," Colleen confirmed. Her hands remained on Molly's shoulders. Her eyes studied Molly's waist.

Molly sniffed, hard. The rose odor was so faint. The collar smelled mostly of cedar now. "I wasn't even three," she said sadly.

"You were very small," Colleen agreed. "Here, take this off." She set aside Mama's dress and began to pull the dyed Mother Hubbard over Molly's head. Now, in the mirror, Molly was a girl diminished to white chemise and drawers. She looked better in white than in black. Behind her, deeper into the reflection, Colleen was rummaging through her own wardrobe, pushing aside dyed-black wool, calico, chintz and lawn. She found what she wanted. "Put your arms out." She wound a corset around Molly's middle. "Hold your breath."

A corset? Colleen thought Molly was old enough for a corset? Obediently, Molly sucked in her waist. She looked down at her very small chest and began to feel almost cheerful. Maybe her figure wasn't quite ready, but any girl who had almost had her first kiss was ready for … "Oomph!" Molly lost all of her air. "Does it have to be so tight?" she squeaked.

Colleen didn't answer. She was too busy turning the bodice of the gray dress inside-out, examining its seams, removing most of the boning. Molly breathed, watching herself in the mirror, experimenting. She was most successful with shallow intakes, air that dropped no lower than her throat.

"Am *I* going to wear Mama's dress?" she panted.

"If I can make it fit," Colleen promised.

Molly inhaled all the way down to her breastbone. This was a momentous occasion, entirely unexpected. A corset and a long skirt meant a girl had finally entered into womanhood!

But Colleen didn't seem to want to talk. She just measured and manipulated. She dressed Molly as if Molly were a doll, lifting Molly's arms to slide on the bodice, pushing Molly's head forward to fasten the long row of hooks up the back. With pins from her pincushion, she sized the bodice down in the front and out on the sides. Then she helped Molly step through the waistband of the skirt. "Good," she said. To herself, not to Molly. "Too big in the waist, but long enough." She stood back to study the result. "I'll have to add length to the sleeves, though," she mused.

Molly wriggled her hips. Just a little, just enough to make the skirt swish. It felt strange, but wonderful, to have cloth touching her ankles. An inside-out woman looked back at her from the mirror. "Am I going to wear this to *school?*" she asked. Amy would die of envy.

"Not to school." Colleen was measuring the length of Molly's wrist. She spoke through the pins in her mouth. "I have a plan. I haven't yet told you – I wasn't sure it would work. But now I think it will do very well."

A few hours later, back in her black Mother Hubbard, Molly drooped wearily over a table in Cooper's Drugstore. Amy, her oldest and best friend, chattered at her side. Amy always chattered. Jonathan, the true love of Molly's life, was silent except for the slurping of his chocolate milkshake. Jonathan was almost always silent.

Molly glanced up from her bowl of vanilla ice cream so that she could memorize for forever their two dear faces. She broke into Amy's monologue, uttering the awful words, "Colleen and I are moving."

Amy frowned. Then her brow cleared. "Well, that house is awful big for just the two of you," she said comfortingly. "I'm sure you can find something smaller. Something just as pleasant. Why, I've heard that Widow Horne is going up to Chicago to live with her daughter, and that means that her house –"

Molly turned pleading eyes to Jonathan. He didn't notice. He seemed very satisfied with his milkshake.

"Away!" This time Molly wailed. "Colleen and I are going to Chicago too!"

Amy was startled. She said only one word, "Why?"

Jonathan spoke up. "Chicago's one hundred miles from here."

"We know our geography," Amy snapped. "Explain, Molly."

Molly tried to explain as Colleen had done. "We're poor." It was an amazing fact. "Papa was ill for so long, all our money was used up. Colleen had to pay the doctor and the druggist and the mortician. For months now, we've been living on a loan from the bank. The bank owns our house."

Jonathan's face took on an almost-adult expression of horror. "A loan!" he exclaimed. He was shocked, but at the wrong disaster. "Pa don't hold with loans."

"Shut up," Amy ordered him. "Why Chicago, Molly?"

"Because we have to have jobs." This was another amazing fact, one that Molly couldn't yet believe. "Colleen says we can't earn a living here in Streator. She's been saving this." Molly handed Amy a scrap of newspaper.

Amy read the advertisement out loud. "*Young women of good character, attractive and intelligent, eighteen to thirty, to work in Harvey Eating Houses.*" She appraised Molly. "You're only thirteen."

"I can be eighteen in Chicago where nobody knows me," Molly explained. "That's what Colleen says." That's what the dove-gray dress had been all about.

"Well, let Colleen go to Chicago." Amy was decisive. "You can come live with me."

"Really?" The possibility was a lifeline.

"I'll go home right now and speak to Mama." Amy pushed back her chair. "Coming, Jonathan?"

Jonathan waited until Amy was almost to the door. Then he also stood, speaking his fourth phrase of the afternoon: "I don't want you to leave." He reddened.

Molly basked in the warmth of Jonathan's blush until her bowl of ice cream had melted into a beige, speckled soup. Could she really move her six dyed Mother Hubbards from her own wardrobe to Amy's? Start the eighth grade with her friends? Kiss Jonathan behind the big oak?

Why ever not?!

But first, Colleen would have to agree. Molly would have to argue so clearly, so persuasively, so convincingly, that Colleen would be unable to resist. Walking along the bricks of Main Street, Molly rehearsed. Amy's mother had grown up with Mama. Papa had often described Amy's father as "admirable." Amy was almost like another sister. Colleen could rest assured that Molly would be well taken care of.

"Colleen!" she called, as soon as she opened the front door.

Colleen was up in Papa's room, sorting.

"Colleen," Molly gasped, having taken the stairs two at a time.

"I'm saving a few things for you." Colleen pointed to a small collection on Papa's bed.

"Thank you. I have an idea …" Molly began.

"Like this." Colleen held out a small leather bag.

Molly had to postpone her speech. She took the bag, loosened the ties, and turned it upside down.

Papa's gold watch slid into her palm.

Molly's heart slowed, as if she hadn't just charged up a

flight of stairs. Carefully, gently, she pried open the watch's front cover to read for the thousandth time what was engraved inside: "Time Marches On." It was Papa's favorite saying.

"I thought the watch should go to you," Colleen said. "You used to love playing with it when you were small. Remember?"

Molly remembered. She used to "steal" the watch while Papa pretended not to notice. Molly's fingers would creep across Papa's front, dip into his waistcoat pocket and then pull the watch out to the fullest length of its chain. Sometimes, Molly "stole" the watch while Papa was working in his mercantile. Then all the customers would join in the laughter. Their joyful noise would rise above the shelves, circle the brooms, dunk in amongst the pickles.

That had all happened so very long ago.

"I'm grateful to have you, Molly." Colleen's voice dropped to almost a whisper. "I think I would be unbearably sad otherwise."

"Oh!" And suddenly Molly's excellent arguments for staying in Streator lost all significance. She plopped down on the bed beside Colleen. She looked around at the open drawers, the cleared dresser top, the empty wardrobe – all signs of irreversible change. "I hate this."

Colleen nodded. "It's terribly hard."

Molly pulled up her feet to sit cross-legged. She watched her sister continue to sort. A pile for Papa's collars, a pile for his bow ties. Most of Papa's ties were green, like his eyes had been. Nobody in the whole world had eyes exactly like Papa's. Except for Colleen.

✦ ⁓ᢒᡦ⁓ ✦

Jonathan's father arrived after lunch the next day. Molly recognized the wagon. It was the one with a new axle, the one that had carried her class on so many school outings. The bed was large enough to hold a dozen bales of hay, but she and Colleen had only two valises. Two valises were all that was left of their Streator lives.

"Ready?" Jonathan's father asked.

"We are," Colleen answered.

Colleen and Amy had fussed over Molly for ages. Now Amy presented Molly like a show-and-tell. Molly wore Mama's dress with the corset much too tight underneath. Her hair was piled on top of her head, like a lady's. Colleen had skewered a red-feathered gray hat over Molly's topknot, fastening it firmly with a six-inch-long pin.

Jonathan's eyebrows rose.

"Sit right there." Amy bustled Molly onto the bench seat next to Jonathan.

"Gee up," Jonathan's father told the horses.

Molly tried to twist around so that she could say goodbye to her house, to the neighbors' houses, to that empty lot on the corner where she and Amy had long ago pretended to be African explorers. But she couldn't turn because of the corset. She had to face front. The wagon wheels jerked up onto Main

Street. All the shopkeepers, all of Papa's friends, came out of their stores to wave. *Goodbye, goodbye, goodbye.* Molly waved back.

The horses ceased clip-clopping on brick. Their hooves thudded more softly on hardened dirt. Colleen and Jonathan's father spoke about the weather, about the upcoming harvest, about Jonathan's grandmother's bad knee. Molly silently bade farewell to the mayor's corn fields, the doctor's old mule, and the sorghum shack where all of Streator gathered for the autumn festival. She gulped down a sob.

Amy put her arm around Molly's shoulders.

"You look real pretty," Jonathan said, from Molly's other side.

Amy dropped her arm so that she could poke Molly in the ribs, hard. Molly could almost feel Amy's elbow through the corset. *He complimented you!* Amy's elbow blared. But what Amy said out loud was, "You'll write, won't you? Tell us what you're doing, what it's like? You'll be a Chicago girl now, Molly!"

Molly tried to nod, but her hair and hat made nodding painful. The corset allowed no slouching. She knew she looked firmer than she felt, sitting on that wagon seat, and then standing, a half hour later, next to Colleen at the train stop.

"Best of luck," said Jonathan's father.

"Thank you," Colleen replied.

Jonathan thrust a gift wrapped in leftover calico into

Molly's hands.

"Not goodbye, just till later!" Amy hugged her.

Molly stumbled getting up onto the train. She was pathetically grateful to the stranger who helped her, who had the courtesy to watch without a smile while she extricated herself from a tangle of skirt and shoes, who sat down beside her and pretended not to notice her tears.

She touched the tip of her nose to the window.

"Don't forget to write! We'll miss you!" Amy shouted, and Molly knew that this was another picture she would hold forever in her mind and in her heart. Her best, her most loyal friends, Amy and Jonathan, standing close together, waving goodbye.

Chapter 2

"The far West is a magnet attracting the most lawless
of society ..." *Billy the Kid and Company*

Jonathan's parting gift was his favorite book, *Billy the
Kid and Company*. Molly had seen him read it everywhere:
balanced on a make-shift bar set between plow handles;
hidden beneath his desk at school; propped on his knees
while he leaned against a tree. Jonathan had been reading and
rereading *Billy the Kid and Company* ever since he was short
and squeaky. It was, he once told their class during show-and-
tell, the most wonderful book in the world.

And he had given it to her.

Colleen didn't watch while Molly unfolded the calico

wrapping. She appeared caught in her own thoughts, probably about the weather, or the harvest, or something else that didn't have much feeling. But the man who sat beside Molly, the man who had helped her onto the train, smiled. He angled his face to include Colleen in his smile. Colleen transferred her gaze toward the empty aisle. Ladies traveling alone didn't talk to strange men.

Molly held the book to her cheek for a long moment before returning it to her lap. The cover was water-stained, and one corner was ripped away. The page edges were dark with prairie soil. She placed a hand on the dear, dear cover and stroked it, like a precious pet. Reading, she would feel closer to Jonathan. Reading, she ventured into the dangers of the far, far West. The stories were an escape from what had happened to Papa, what would happen in Chicago, why she was on this train.

Then the man stood up, his tailored legs swaying with the jerky slowing down of the train. He lowered a big black salesman's case onto his seat. Colleen stayed put, waiting until the train was fully stopped before she gestured to Molly. Molly rose to pull down her own valise. The man, who had been polishing his eyeglasses, popped them back on so that he could help.

"Here you are, Miss? Madam?" He addressed Colleen.

"Thank you." Colleen was properly courteous, properly curt. "Take the lunch basket and your valise," she instructed Molly. She waited while the salesman stood politely aside, then disembarked.

Molly trailed behind her sister. This wasn't her first time in the Chicago depot, so she was only partially impressed. She knew she would become even less so as the minutes wore on. But the initial impact was always overwhelming, with dozens of trains rumbling, hundreds of porters shouting, thousands of passengers pushing. Colleen beckoned, impatient, and Molly hurried: down the platform; into the waiting room where voices collected below the high ceiling like thunder; out to a road tangled with horses, carts, carriages, streetcars, and more people. A *paved* road. Chicago possessed hundreds of paved roads, and even the shortest was much longer than Streator's Main Street.

Molly stopped to wait for a streetcar. On her previous trips to Chicago, she and Papa had always taken streetcars. But Colleen was still walking, consulting the newspaper notice. "This way," Colleen said.

Left. Left again. Right for a very long time. Molly's valise became uncomfortably heavy. She allowed it to touch the street, then bump over the pavement. The corner was rubbed away by the time Colleen finally stopped. Their destination was a building five stories high and pushed to extreme thinness by the nearness of its neighbors. There was room for only one window on each floor, and each window displayed a sign. Colleen's head tilted back as she read the signs on the first, second, then third floor.

"This is it." She turned to Molly. "This is where we ask for work. I'm going to do all the talking. You will smile and say, 'Yes.' Nothing more than that. Do you understand?"

"Yes," Molly agreed.

Colleen took a deep breath. She fussed with her skirt and hair, then marched to the door and turned the knob. Inside, the building smelled of cooked cabbage and mustard. The odor faded by the second floor landing, and on the third floor it was replaced by the gentler scent of Earl Grey tea. Colleen rapped at the windowed door that was stenciled, *Fred Harvey Employment Office*.

"Come in."

It was a woman's voice, the kind that brooked no nonsense. The woman herself sat ruler-straight behind a small desk. It was she who had been enjoying the Earl Grey tea. A dainty teapot and one china cup were set before her. "Yes?" she inquired. She didn't invite the sisters to sit down. There were no chairs for them anyway.

Molly lowered the valise carefully. This woman wasn't the kind who would tolerate a scratch on her floor.

Colleen took another deep breath. Her voice wavered. "We've come about the notice." She stepped forward to put the newspaper clipping next to the teapot. She stepped back.

"Yes?" This Fred Harvey woman seemed to be as word-limited as Molly had been instructed to be. She only glanced at the clipping.

"My sister and I are in need of employment." Colleen had better control of her voice now. "I am Colleen Gerry; I am nineteen years old and in very good health. My sister Molly is eighteen years old. I have completed my education. Molly was forced to leave after the seventh grade, but she is a very bright girl."

The Harvey woman observed Molly. Molly did her best to look bright. The Harvey woman inclined her head. "Tall girls are often quite strong," she allowed. "Mr. Harvey demands hard work and *exemplary* conduct." She underlined, italicized, and otherwise made a point with the word.

Molly switched from looking bright to looking exemplary.

"I've never even been engaged!" Colleen blurted.

The woman tapped her fingernail against the teapot. Chink, chink, chink. "I will send you to Raton," she declared.

Colleen exhaled as if she had been holding her breath for weeks. "Oh, thank you!" she gushed.

Molly searched her mind for some forgotten geography lesson that mentioned a Chicago suburb called Raton.

"The Harvey Houses have made the Atchison, Topeka and Santa Fe one of the top railway lines," the woman lectured.

Raton must be close by the depot.

"We have Harvey restaurants all the way from Topeka, Kansas to San Bernardino, California."

And in Raton, Illinois.

"You can catch the 4 p.m. to Kansas City. You will change trains and get your uniforms there. Raton is our first stop in New Mexico."

"New Mexico?" The words escaped Molly's mouth. They

were so foreign, so impossible, they had to be said out loud.

"It will be wonderful, won't it, Molly?" Colleen said hastily.

"You will room and board at the Harvey House." The woman opened her desk drawer to remove two slips of paper. She handed the slips to Colleen along with a book. "These are your train passes. The Atchison, Topeka and Santa Fe Railway gives this guidebook to all its passengers who are going the distance. The best of luck to you." She stood, a signal that the sisters should leave her office.

Colleen touched Molly's shoulder. Molly turned to go, but she let her valise drag. She no longer cared if it gouged this woman's over-polished floor.

"New Mexico!" she said on the landing.

"Hush," Colleen hissed.

"*New Mexico!*" Molly bumped her valise down the stairs.

"It's for the best," Colleen replied.

"You said we would be working in Chicago!"

"I didn't know for sure."

"I thought we'd go home and visit for Christmas!"

"That won't be possible."

Molly stopped. She and Colleen stood outside now, their argument a show for all passersby. "I won't go!"

"We have jobs," Colleen said. "This is good, Molly. Very good. Please try to understand."

"You should have warned me," Molly shouted. "You could have asked!"

And then Colleen lost her temper – something that rarely happened, but always to great effect. "We don't have a world of choices!" she shouted back.

It was as if the earth opened up beneath Molly, as if she were falling not just past horrible New Mexico, but all the way to China, beyond China, into the planet's nighttime sky, out into an anchorless void.

"I didn't want to trouble you." Colleen was back to being cool and collected. "I couldn't know for sure we'd be hired. I certainly didn't know where they would send us. Molly, after paying off Papa's debts, I have less than eighteen dollars in my handbag. Those jobs in Raton are our only future."

> ❄✦❄ ‹

Normally, Molly would have been excited about traveling in a sleeping car. This was her first time to see the facing seats turned into a bed, a shelf pulled down from above to make a bunk. But tonight she had no desire to discuss novelties. Since she had been consulted about nothing, she would discuss nothing. Nothing at all. Colleen had all the power. Colleen had all the plans. When the Pullman porter brought the sisters their pillows and blankets, Molly merely indicated with her hand that she would take the upper berth.

"If that's what you want," Colleen sighed.

Molly had to climb, in her long skirt, using the arms of the seat as a kind of ladder. She sat down with a thump, bouncing the shelf-bunk. Colleen, below, must be ducking, but she didn't complain. She merely stood to pull the draperies around them for privacy. "Do you need help?" she asked. Her nose was level with Molly's waist.

Molly disdained to answer. Colleen's eyes rolled toward the iron ceiling of the sleeping car. Her face sank out of sight.

Molly unbuttoned her shoes, positioning them in a corner where they rattled noisily enough to keep anybody beneath awake for hours. She was forced to remove her skirt while sitting, which meant thumping her bottom up and down and making the shelf bend like a spring. When she struggled out of her corset, she released her imprisoned breath with a loud, torturous groan. Then she lay down. The Pullman pillow smelled of someone else's hair pomade, which was so disgusting, she yelped.

"What?" Colleen's voice rose in alarm.

Molly flung the pillow to the floor in reply. Now she had no place to rest her head save for Jonathan's book. Jonathan's dear, dear book! Her tears added new stains to the cover. *Billy the Kid and Company* was a testimony of Molly's loss, a history of her love.

She mourned with her eyes wide open, and then she mourned with her eyes unwillingly shut. She had meant to stay awake, to suffer a lingering farewell for each familiar town that the conductor called out, but somehow she fell asleep. And when Colleen shook her shoulder, the car was lit with gas lamps, and the other passengers were making dressing noises in their cubicles.

Colleen began issuing orders. "Put on your clothes. Tidy your hair." She plucked Jonathan's book from where it had wandered and dropped it into the empty lunch basket. "Hurry."

Molly hurried, sort of. She made a vague attempt at tidying. She lowered herself to the aisle with a thud. "Let me," said Colleen, and she seized Molly's hair, which flew about Molly's face and fell in strands down Molly's back. "Straighten your skirt," Colleen commanded, which was hard to do without bending one's neck, and impossible to do when somebody else was pulling one's head backward. "Are you ready?"

The word *No!* boiled in Molly's mouth. It pushed hotly against her lips. But she didn't let it escape.

"Kansas City!" the conductor called. Colleen gave up on Molly's hair. She herded Molly down the aisle, off the train, and into a station almost as large as Chicago's. She asked official-looking people for directions and then she grabbed Molly's hand. She pulled Molly all the way through the depot, outside onto a Kansas City street that Molly hardly saw, and then back inside the depot through a much smaller entrance. She didn't seem bothered by Molly's silence. She seemed not to notice it at all.

This entrance was topped with a golden, crown-shaped sign. The awful words, *Harvey Company*, were painted in black where a head should have been. Colleen marched down the hallway as if she belonged there. She stopped in front of an open door and announced herself. "Good morning."

"Good morning," returned an elderly gentleman. He was balanced on a ladder leaning against a huge, lined blackboard. Each line began with the name of a town. He was at *Topeka* level, writing *lobsters* next to *ice*. "You are?" he inquired.

"Colleen and Molly Gerry," said Colleen.

"Ah, yes! We've had a telegram about you. Welcome to the Harvey family, my dears! Forgive me for not coming down, but I don't move as well as I used to. Go back out into the hallway and open the first door on your right." He waved his chalk-holding hand. "Take what you need. You'll see a list on the wall."

"Thank you. Come, Molly."

Molly came, like a puppy on a leash. She entered a room filled with black and white clothing. "Two of each," Colleen read from the list on the wall. She held a black skirt and bodice up against herself, then did the same to Molly. "Look through those aprons. Pick four that are long enough."

Molly, as obedient as a trained but reluctant dog, pawed through the white aprons.

"I'll have to narrow your waistbands," Colleen murmured. "And hem my skirts. Why didn't I think to bring my sewing basket?"

Molly, grudgingly, pointed to a wide windowsill loaded with sewing supplies.

"Perfect! I wonder if we can take these scissors with us?" Colleen darted next door to ask.

Molly heard the question and then the reply. "Of course, my dear. That's what they're there for. And be sure to take four collars. That's what Mr. Harvey now orders. Four collars each. I have yet to change the sign."

"Eight collars," Colleen called.

Molly grabbed additional collars without counting. She waited for what Colleen would do to her next. Colleen walked, pleased, back into the garment room and made Molly hold out her arms. She loaded Molly up with black and white clothing. She collected thread and needles from the windowsill.

Molly could no longer contain herself. She had to speak. And whatever she said would have to be so large, so big, Colleen would have no choice but to listen. Molly mined her brain for words powerful enough to stop Colleen in her tracks. She thought hard and deep – which was difficult to do because Colleen was now towing her back through the depot to their next train.

They were the first to board. They had all the seats to choose from. Colleen fussed, selecting seats, packing their new uniforms into the lunch basket. She handed *Billy the Kid and Company* to Molly as if it were a space-grabbing, worthless item.

"Now!" Colleen settled herself down as if she had completed a job with excellent results and deserved a rest. She opened her Atchison, Topeka and Santa Fe guidebook to read aloud. "*Kansas City is the gateway to the West, and the state* motto of Missouri exemplifies the goal of all our territories: *The Welfare of the People Shall Be the Supreme Law.* That's the kind of place we're going to, Molly."

Molly finally knew what to say. She knew exactly where to find the perfect response. She opened *Billy the Kid and Company*, Chapter One, *Desperados*. She read out loud in a strong, book-authoritative voice. "*The far West is a magnet attracting the most lawless of society: escaped convicts, murderers, horse thieves.*"

Colleen didn't blanch. Instead, she shuffled pages too. She read, "*Many great men have called Missouri home, including Mark Twain.*"

Molly countered. "*Even the names of the Western desperados evoke fear: Rattlesnake Sam, Hoodoo Brown, Cockeyed Frank, Web-fingered Billy, Quick-knife Nance.*"

"*Stories of Western conflict are greatly exaggerated,*" Colleen quoted.

Molly had to stop. She could no longer continue the exchange. Her intention had been to frighten Colleen, but instead she was alarming herself. Other passengers were now entering the car. Was that man's name simple and civilized, like John Jones? Or did he call himself something horrible, like Murderous Mike? Did he, did the other passengers, carry hidden weapons beneath their jackets or inside their shoes? How was Molly Gerry, an average girl from Streator, Illinois, supposed to distinguish the notorious from the ordinary?

The train moved, and Molly had to move too. She was

too anxious to sit still. She rose, ignoring Colleen's, "Molly?" and stumbled all the way down their car and into the next. The train lurched. Molly's heart lurched too, but with relief. She recognized a big black salesman's case, then spectacles on an otherwise nondescript face. The train completed its swing around a curve, and Molly grabbed the back of the man's seat. He looked up from his newspaper.

Molly collapsed into the seat opposite him. "Hello," she said.

"Hello?" He didn't seem to recognize her.

"We haven't met properly." The words gushed out. "And Colleen would say that it's forward of me to introduce myself to you now. But you got on the same train to Chicago that we did, near Streator, Illinois. You're the only person I almost-know in the entire West. I'm Molly Gerry."

"Hugh Latterly, at your service." Mr. Latterly half-rose, making this introduction both more polite and almost-official.

"I'm traveling with my sister." Molly tried to spark some recognition. "Colleen."

"Oh." Comprehension lit Mr. Latterly's face. "The lovely young woman with the hazel eyes!"

"I don't know how you can admire her," Molly said bitterly. "Ever since Papa became ill, she's looked like an old maid."

"I hope your father has recovered." Mr. Latterly's response was courteous.

Molly touched the lump in her waist pocket that was

Papa's watch. She spoke over the lump that rose in her throat. "He died."

"I'm so sorry."

"Thank you." Molly swallowed the lump down. "Did you know Papa?" she asked. "Did you know his store in Streator? It was called Gerry Mercantile. It's called Thompson Mercantile, now."

"I'm sorry, I don't know that store," Mr. Latterly apologized. "I've only been on this route for a few months. I sell eyeglasses. See?" He opened his case to display row after row of shining lenses. "Would you – or would your sister – be in need of a pair?"

"No," said Molly, "we both see very well."

Mr. Latterly closed his case. He pressed the clasp to make sure it was tight. "We should be coming into Kansas just about now," he remarked.

There was no boundary outside the window that Molly could see, no line of demarcation that meant she was entering a state she had never been inclined to visit. Her homesickness surged, hugely and overwhelmingly. "Colleen will be wondering about me." She excused herself.

On the tiny platform between the two cars, she paused. She inhaled – or tried to. They grew corn in Kansas too. But her nose filled with the odors of tar and rotten eggs – coal smoke.

When she reached Colleen, she flung herself down on the seat. She avoided Colleen's questioning eyebrows. She gazed out the window, trying to not-see. She imagined: those were Illinois cornfields; the train had miraculously turned around; she was going home. But her daydream was punctured by the conductor, who came down the aisle shouting, "Topeka soon! What's your choice for dinner? Dining room or lunch counter?"

Molly knew nothing about Topeka. Her class had never studied Kansas geography. Probably even their teacher didn't know how many countless miles Topeka was from Streator.

"Counter," Colleen told the conductor.

When the train stopped at a small depot, in the midst of fields that were much too dry, they were met by a man who banged a gong as if he wanted to awaken all the prairie dead. "Follow me, folks!" he cried. Still banging, he ushered the passengers into a restaurant. "Counter to the right, dining room to the left," he yelled above his own clamor.

Colleen veered right, so Molly did too. There were more people than stools at the counter, but those who were served ate fast. Whenever a stool opened up, the crowd pushed forward. "Chicken salad! Corned beef! Peach pie!" the passengers shouted. The three waitresses – three black and white Harvey uniforms – took orders and served food with alarming speed.

The crowd shoved Molly up to a stool. "Coffee? Milk? Tea?" Her waitress smiled as if she had all the time in the world, as if Molly were her only customer.

"Breakfast," Molly said, because Colleen hadn't provided any breakfast that morning.

"Of course."

Molly's request seemed to be no trouble at all. "Pancakes," she clarified. "Oatmeal with honey. Ham. And milk, please."

Her milk arrived instantly, her food only a minute or two later. "Anything else?" the waitress inquired.

"No."

The waitress was off to serve somebody else. Colleen slid onto the next stool over. "Watch," she commanded Molly. "Learn."

Watch and learn *what*? Molly mostly ate. All the while her waitress cleared dishes, poured coffee, and cut pie. The young woman accomplished more in a half hour than Molly had ever accomplished in a day. By the time the man with the gong began banging again, by the time he called out, "Time to get back on board, folks," Molly was exhausted. Not by the food or the noise, but by her waitress's Herculean efforts.

"We can't do that, Colleen."

"We – *you* – are perfectly capable," Colleen stated with unarguable certainty.

Returned to the train, Molly needed to talk with somebody, anybody – Amy most of all. But the only soul she knew was Mr. Latterly. He was exactly where he had been that morning. Molly again took the seat opposite. "My sister says we have to become Harvey waitresses." It was more than a complaint; it was a plea for help.

"The sister with the hazel eyes!" This time Mr. Latterly recognized her.

"She found jobs for us in Raton, New Mexico." Molly made her grief explicit.

Mr. Latterly proved to be absolutely the wrong person to talk to. "The Harvey Girls are the jewels of the West," he enthused. "We'll be having supper in Newton this evening. Perhaps I could join your sister and you? I have stopped in Raton before. I will be happy to tell you all about your new home."

He was a disappointment. A complete and utter disappointment. Molly had no place to go but back to *Billy the Kid and Company*. For the rest of that day's journey she kept her eyes on the book. The countryside beyond was looking less and less like Illinois anyway. Too much wheat, not enough corn. She burrowed herself deep into Chapter Two.

Coming into Newton, Colleen chose the dining room for supper. Another gong, another man yelling directions. Colleen made comments all the way to the table. "White linen. That looks like real silver, Molly, and very good china. They must make every meal a special occasion."

Mr. Latterly elbowed his way toward them. He seized the back of the chair catty-corner to Colleen's. "Miss Gerry." He bowed. "Your sister, Miss Molly, and I met on the train …" The conversation that followed was perfectly meaningless. Colleen and Mr. Latterly chatted about the journey so far, shared observations about the miles past and made predictions about the route to come. Mr. Latterly produced useless fact after useless fact. "The soil is indeed rich here in Kansas, but the land is flat only in appearance. We have gained almost one thousand feet in elevation since Kansas City."

Molly had gained nothing since Topeka but heightened apprehension. She saw nothing around her but promises of disaster. These Newton waitresses were even more rushed than the Topeka counter girls had been. Still, somehow, smoothly, almost gliding, they flew through the patterns of their work. One waitress took orders, another poured drinks. Molly's fruit cup disappeared to be replaced by a red fish in a dill sauce.

"Salmon," Colleen marveled.

"Brought all the way from Washington Territory," Mr. Latterly expounded.

He was a pompous, over-informed show-off. He had eaten in Harvey Restaurants all the way to California. He called Harvey Girls "bold and enterprising young women." He had no proper sense of doom.

"The West is the most perilous place in the United States of America." Molly broke into his monologue. She quoted, or almost quoted, from *Billy the Kid and Company*. "Sixteen out of every one hundred people suffer a violent demise." She wasn't exactly sure of the true number, but sixteen was close enough to what she had read to be real. "Every railroad west of St. Louis has been robbed *multiple* times." She was certain of that fact.

"With the most successful robber of them all being Genius Jim," Mr. Latterly added genially.

"Yes!" Molly was both surprised and grateful for his

support. She amplified: "Genius Jim is the most wanted criminal in New Mexico, Colleen. He dynamited a train in Silver City and got away with $100,000. Six people *died*." She pronounced the last word with dire emphasis.

"That's enough!" Colleen insisted. She turned to Mr. Latterly. "My sister sometimes frightens herself," she explained.

Molly sank back in her chair. The Harvey waitresses offered seconds and thirds. They whisked away plates and returned with dessert. The everlasting gong sounded; the depot man intoned, "That's it, folks."

Mr. Latterly opened his watch. "One half hour, exactly," he said with satisfaction. "It is truly amazing what these Harvey Girls can do."

Molly wasn't amazing. She was only ordinary. Maybe even less than ordinary. She followed Colleen and Mr. Latterly back to the train, but she didn't reclaim her seat. Instead, she took herself through car after car to the very end. She had thought she might linger on the very last platform and gaze forlornly eastward, wiping tears from her eyes. But the last car was a gentlemen's lounge, impassable for women. She was forced to return to her sister.

"I hope you're not still worrying, Miss Molly," Mr. Latterly said, when she lurched by.

Molly was too dispirited to answer.

"You're perfectly safe." He was back in information-delivering mode. "There are four men I'm convinced are plain-clothes detectives sitting in the gent's lounge right now. And two detectives and an ATSF rifleman in the express car behind the coal bin. I've ridden on this train countless times, and I've never been robbed."

"Maybe you've been lucky," Molly sighed.

Mr. Latterly reached for his black case. "Perhaps this would ease your mind. I wouldn't normally sell this item. But for you, for your sister …" The case must have had another, invisible latch, because the wrong side fell open, revealing an unexpected compartment beneath the spectacles. The space was filled with handkerchiefs. Mr. Latterly rummaged through them until he found a golden four-leaf clover. He pressed the clover into Molly's palm. "My lucky pendant. It saved my life once."

Molly definitely needed to have her life saved. "How much?" she asked.

"Five dollars."

Molly rubbed the metal. The clover had a deep dent in the middle, as if someone had hammered it with a rod. She brought the pendant close to her eyes. "Brass," Papa's daughter declared. Molly hadn't spent her childhood in a mercantile for nothing. "Not gold. I'll give you five cents."

"I can't take less than a dollar, Molly. It means so much to me."

Molly had seen Papa handle dozens – no, hundreds – of salesmen just like Mr. Latterly. "Seven cents," she offered.

"At least a half dollar!" he exclaimed. "It was a gift from my old mother!"

"Eight cents," and there Molly held firm.

Mr. Latterly finally accepted. Papa would have been proud. Molly was certainly proud – until she realized she had no money.

"You may take it on credit," Mr. Latterly was more than accommodating, he was eager, "if you tell me something about your sister."

Molly didn't know what to say.

"Does she have a beau? Is she musical? Does she like to dance?" Mr. Latterly asked.

"No beau," Molly revealed. She considered the other questions. They belonged to who Colleen had been before Papa became ill. "Mostly," said Molly, "she's useful."

→ ⋅⊰⊱⋅ ←

The next morning, Mr. Latterly continued his attentions to Colleen. They all ate their breakfasts together at a dining table in La Junta, Colorado. This dining room was almost identical to the one in Newton. And Molly's choices – pancakes, oatmeal, and ham – tasted exactly the same as the food in Topeka.

"I must continue on to Denver," Mr. Latterly informed Colleen, "but I will be in New Mexico in a month or so. I hope you will allow me to call on you."

"Of course." Colleen was more polite than encouraging. Exactly one half hour later, after saying goodbye to Mr. Latterly on the La Junta depot platform, she appeared to forget him entirely. She re-opened her guidebook. She perused a few pages and then read out loud. "*From La Junta, Colorado, we enter a part of our country that is so different as to be almost foreign. With no need to cross a great ocean, we are in a mysterious and exciting land.*"

Molly allowed Colleen to read on uninterrupted because, in spite of herself, she was interested. She listened as she looked. The funny huts outside the window were adobe houses. The women in bright skirts were Mexican. The train picked up speed. The women's skirts flitted by like butterflies. Molly got up on her knees so that she could more fully face the window.

"Sit like a lady." Colleen tugged Molly back down.

The train twisted and turned into a country of rocks and pines. The ride became too jerky for Colleen to continue reading. The landscape outside the window would have been stark, even dreary, except for the streams that flowed fast and clear. The rivers that Molly had known before were muddy. These streams sparkled. They threw out flashes of light. Molly, holding onto the window rim, could feel the great power of the engines pulling the train upward. Now the streams no longer flowed, they fell. "A waterfall!" she exclaimed.

"A waterfall!" Colleen leaned past her to share the marvel.

Steam and smoke trailed past the window. The countryside disappeared, but only for a minute or two. When the murkiness cleared, Molly looked up and up to see a yellow cliff that was higher than ten silos stacked one on top of the other. The mountains in Illinois were only hills, she now realized – little bumps of dirt and grass. These Colorado mountains looked as if they could pierce heaven.

"*It was the Indians, in times immemorial, who discovered Raton Pass.*" Colleen was back to the guide book.

Molly opened the window so she could stick her head out. The train turned. She caught a glimpse of mountains that went on forever, the most distant ones blued by haze and topped by what she could only guess was snow. The train turned again, this time chugging into its own smoke.

Colleen coughed. They were entering the suffocating darkness of a tunnel now. The engines labored. Molly sat very still, looking ahead into nothing. The voices of the people in the nearby seats sounded nervous. But soon a circle of daylight appeared, and Molly's shoulders could relax. The train was back in the sunshine, laboring to stop itself from speeding downhill. The conductor entered the car.

"Welcome to New Mexico, folks!" he boomed.

Chapter 3

"Western hospitality is replete with smiles." *The Atchison, Topeka and Santa Fe Railway Guidebook*

They stepped off the train into a strong and persistent sunlight that made Molly squint. Just as at the other stops, a man sounded a gong, but this time Colleen didn't follow the gong toward dinner. Instead, she remained on the wooden platform, the valises at her feet. "This is where it matters, Molly," she said. "Do exactly what I do. Act eighteen!"

The other travelers followed the guide. This Raton depot almost exactly matched La Junta's depot – and Newton's and Topeka's – even down to the old men sitting on a platform bench, holding out their watches, timing the train. But at this stop, two uniformed girls and a young woman in fine blue silk emerged from the adjacent restaurant and pushed their way against the tide of passengers. The young woman in silk snatched her dress up from the ground as soon as she got out of the crush, and sprinted.

Even so, it was one of the uniforms who reached Molly and Colleen first. This girl was taller than most men. Her legs, beneath all that black and white, must have been enormously long. "Welcome!" she said.

The blue silk girl caught up. Beneath her finery, her shoes were thick and practical, her stockings black and mended. The hem of her dress, looped over her arm, was unfinished and raw-cut, the fabric shedding bits of thread. "Hello!"

Finally, the second uniform arrived. "I'm Nell," she introduced herself.

"Faye," said blue silk.

"Annis." The one with long legs picked up both valises.

They surrounded Molly and Colleen like a friendly human wall, steering them to the restaurant's far side. Molly glimpsed a street and a line of clapboard structures, then she was up on a porch and Faye was urging her, "Go on in."

Molly stepped into a kitchen which was large, but crowded. And noisy! Immediately, she pressed her back against a staircase so as to be out of the way.

"*Non! Non! Non!*" A chef in a tall white hat was making most of the noise. White-shirted assistants revolved around him. Harvey Girls came in and out of a swinging door, pushing carts, carrying trays. Everybody rushed, everybody was busy, but nobody collided. Chef, assistants, Harvey Girls – they were all dancing an intricate, complicated kitchen reel, as if they knew it by heart.

Molly felt dizzy.

"This way." Faye guided her around the stairs, into a sitting room beyond. "Sit down, do." She cleared a space on a long table, pushing aside scraps of blue silk, tape, lace and a bustle covered in white flounces. "This is our lounge."

"I'll bring your dinner." Annis, the long-legged girl, disappeared.

Colleen sat down next to Molly, and Molly remembered. She was supposed to imitate her sister. She folded her hands on her lap. She tried to arrange a smile on her face. She murmured, "Thank you," when Annis returned with a tray. Their dinner was a casserole of chicken in a red sauce, potato soufflé, green beans with almonds, and walnut pie.

Nell lingered by the door, half going, half staying. "Where're you from?" she asked.

"Streator, Illinois," Colleen answered.

"I'm an Iowa girl, myself," said Nell. "Ready to scoot, Annis?"

"I'm from Ohio," said Annis, before scooting.

Faye remained. "We're all from different states. I'm from New Jersey. Go ahead, eat. Our chef is the best on the line."

Colleen picked up her fork. "My!" she politely exclaimed. "This is delicious."

Molly picked up her fork too. The chicken was more than delicious – it was amazing. She held that first bite in her mouth, tasting, savoring. Wine. The red sauce was made from a red wine.

"How many girls work here?" Colleen asked.

"Nine right now. Although you'll be eight after I leave," Faye answered.

The potato soufflé was as light as angel food cake. No, lighter, because it wasn't as stiff.

"Who's in charge?"

"Mr. Thomas is our General Manager, but we girls answer to Miss Lambert."

The walnut pie … No, Molly had never tasted this nut before. Walnuts were musty and dry, this nut was buttery and almost sweet.

"Finished?" Faye asked, because Colleen was, even though Molly was not. Obediently, she abandoned her dinner to follow Faye and Colleen up the stairs, down a hallway of shut doors and into the very last room. She had to blink, then close her eyes halfway, because of the brightness. Sunbeams were somehow streaming in from two windows and from two directions. "You'll get used to the light," Faye promised. "We have a different sky out here than what you're used to." She pulled the curtains to dim the glare. "Go ahead and unpack and rest. Miss Lambert will find you when the dinner service is over." She started to leave, but then paused to look back over her shoulder. "Miss Lambert's not as fierce as she seems."

The door clicked.

"We're here," Colleen said, a wondering tone in her voice as if she and Molly had just flown over the moon, which perhaps they had.

All the flavors in Molly's mouth – chicken, wine, potato, the mysterious nut – suddenly turned sour. She put her hands over her eyes to shut out the two beds, the wardrobe, the one chair. She wanted to shut out what remained of the light. But even dimmed, the New Mexico sun was inexorable. It pushed through the cracks between Molly's fingers. It filled her closed eyes with its brightness. It forced tears down her cheeks.

"We have to try, Molly," Colleen said quietly. "We have to make Papa proud."

Papa. Papa would have been miserable to see his daughters in a place like this. He had worked so hard to provide, and now everything was gone. Everything, except … Molly dropped one hand to touch the little pocket at her waist. Her fingers pulsed with the familiar tick, tick, tick of Papa's watch. *Time Marches On.*

"Please," Colleen begged.

And for Papa, for Colleen, Molly tried. She chose a bed and a side of the wardrobe. She removed her hat. She unpacked her valise. She clutched *Billy the Kid and Company* to her chest, then slid it beneath her pillow. When the expected knock came at the door, her shoulders jerked.

Colleen took a deep breath.

Their visitor wore cool, cotton lawn, and was at least

thirty years old, if not more. She was a lady of both fashion and obvious common sense. "I am Miss Lambert," she said, making it clear she was to be called nothing less formal than that. "Welcome to the Raton Harvey House. If you follow me, I will show you around."

This time, when Molly traversed the upstairs hallway, she felt the rumble of a train, the rhythm of departure, through her feet. Her whole body, her very bones, yearned. But it was other people going home, not her.

"You will put your empty valises in the box room." Miss Lambert gestured to the side of the building from where the rumbles had come. "That is the balcony door on our left," she gestured again. "My room," was on the right. "My office," on the left. "If you need to see me you will go to my office, never to my room."

"Yes, Miss Lambert," Colleen agreed.

"A few rules," Miss Lambert continued. "No food upstairs. Curfew is at ten p.m. Your uniform will always be neat, your aprons clean. We allow no jewelry."

"Yes, Miss Lambert," Colleen said again.

"Now you will meet the staff."

They descended the stairs in a row, with Molly last. She re-entered the lounge which, this time, was crowded with the manager, the cashier, cooks and Harvey Girls. Colleen smiled and smiled at the introductions. All the names ran together in Molly's mind. *Mr. Thomas-Sissy-Gaston-Jeanette.*

"Be careful! *Mon Dieu!*" Gaston called. "Do not wobble!"

And a girl dressed in simple work clothes, not a uniform, wheeled a tea cart into the room. The cart held a cake that was six layers tall and covered with strawberries. "It is only nothing," Gaston modestly waved away compliments.

Miss Lambert did the honors of cutting and serving. A fair-haired Harvey Girl brought a piece of the cake to Molly. "I'm Violet," she said. "I'll keep reminding you of our names until you get us all sorted out."

Molly nodded. Violet, like the flower. The inside of this cake was strawberries, whipped cream, and a sponge that melted on Molly's tongue like snow.

"We'd get fat if we weren't so busy," Violet laughed.

"Or this girl could get even taller than she is now," said a voice at Molly's side. Molly turned, then had to look down to see a Harvey Girl whose topknot barely reached Molly's shoulder.

"Meet Sissy," Violet sighed, as if Sissy were a problem they all shared.

"Small women are so much more attractive than big ones, don't you agree?" Sissy remarked.

How was Molly supposed to reply to that? She looked for Colleen, but Colleen was on the far side of the room, listening to Miss Lambert.

"Say hello to Iona," Violet urged.

And all the distresses of the last hour, the last days, the last weeks, began to spark like firecrackers along Molly's spine. It wasn't just her shoulders, but her whole body that shook. She shook so violently, she lost her grip on her plate. It tumbled, fell, struck, then shattered against the floor.

"Whoops!" said Nell, and Molly burst into tears.

→ ⋙⋘ ←

It was early, much too early. Molly's fingers, beneath her pillow, tightened on Papa's watch.

"Molly?" Colleen's tap was gentle against the back of Molly's head. Her voice was concerned. "Turn over. Did that chill take? You mustn't be sick!"

Molly turned. Only moments before, she had been standing surrounded by half-grown corn in an unknown field. Snapped-off leaves lay dry and crumbled on the ground. The sun blazed. The cornstalks smelled sharp and scorched.

Colleen's palm was cool and kind against Molly's forehead.

"It isn't a fever." Colleen no longer whispered. "But you're so flushed. Why, you're just hot, Molly! You pulled up too many covers!" In a moment, Molly's blankets were yanked from her body. She opened her eyes to see Colleen bent over her, determination animating every square inch of Colleen's face. "Get up!"

And Molly remembered. Today was their first day as Harvey Girls.

"Those blankets are for winter, not for now," Colleen fussed. "Let's get you dressed." She threw open the curtains so that their room was both lit and shadowed by the weak reach of the morning sun. "Let's see how you look."

Molly put both feet on the floor. She paused, preferring to go back to the dream, to the drought.

"Now!" said Colleen.

Molly pulled on her underclothes. With Colleen's help, she donned the black bodice and skirt. Too soon, she was wearing the bibbed apron and the white collar. Colleen grabbed Molly's hairbrush from the wash stand. With swift, sure fingers she smoothed Molly's hair; she twisted it up into a knot; she pinned it tight. Then she put a surprisingly gentle hand on each side of Molly's face. She presented Molly to her own reflection in the mirror. "See how pretty?" she coaxed.

The girl in the mirror was a stranger. Molly's fingers crept to her waist. The Harvey uniform had no watch pocket. "Can't we pin Papa's watch somewhere?" she begged.

"No jewelry." Colleen was back to being crisp. "It's a rule. Come on." She led Molly out of their room and down the stairs.

Annis and Nell were waiting in the lounge. "Go back to bed," Annis told Colleen. "Dining room girls don't start work until eight."

"I can't sleep!" Colleen replied. "I'm too excited! This is our first day!"

Nell shook her head. "You'll be pooped!"

Annis turned to Molly. "You, Nell and I will work the lunch counter together this week. Afterward, it'll be just you and Nell."

"You'll learn quick as scat!" Nell promised.

"The first thing we do every day," said Annis, "is get our breakfasts."

In the kitchen, a baker was putting a sheet of cinnamon buns into the oven. The strawberry cake girl was squeezing oranges. A boy was stacking clean dishes on the shelves beside the washing sink. The boy and the girl worked with speed and competency, as if they had been working in this kitchen for weeks, or months, or maybe even years. They didn't look any older than Molly's true age. Perhaps their fathers had died too.

"We get our fruit from California," Annis was saying. "Try the juice. You'll love it." She poured from a pitcher.

Molly did love it. For a moment her life became as narrow, as perfect, as the taste and smell of an orange. But, "The breakfast cook will be here soon. If you want something special, he'll make it. Usually, we just take whatever is out," Annis's voice brought her back to the Harvey world.

Molly took boiled eggs, fresh rolls, butter and strawberry jam from a long shelf attached to the dining room wall side of the kitchen. With the others, she carried her meal into the lounge. She had hardly finished before Annis announced, "Almost six!" Behind Annis, after Nell, after Colleen, she stacked her dirty dishes in the kitchen sink.

Colleen put a foot on the staircase. "Good luck, Molly," she said, her expression both anxious and hopeful.

"Wait a moment," said Annis. "I want both of you to look."

Molly looked. She saw her sister, whom she would

50

probably never see again. She saw the kitchen which, no doubt, would soon become a dancing madhouse. She saw the lounge door with a long green curtain hanging beside it. She saw the swinging doors that led into the dining room.

"This is the busiest spot in the entire Harvey House," Annis instructed. "Dining room girls coming in with trays, the kitchen boy going out with clean dishes, the cook bringing food to the lunch counter. Always look before you step here."

"We will," Colleen vowed.

"Now." Annis pushed aside the green curtain, revealing the working side of the lunch counter where cups were hidden on knee-high shelves, and the big coffee urn sat in its own special nook. Molly stepped forward, the green curtain fell shut, and Colleen was gone.

"You'll be in the middle, Molly," said Annis.

So began the most awful morning of Molly's life. From the moment Mr. Thomas, the manager, opened the Harvey House door, the twelve counter chairs were always swiveling to accommodate new customers. "Steak!" "Ham!" "Donuts!" Annis and Nell could listen to three or four orders at once and then push the green curtain aside to call for what they needed. Somebody in the kitchen always heard, and in a few minutes the food would appear, placed on a shelf just inside the counter area.

Molly was supposed to do exactly as Annis and Nell did, but she couldn't. She would hear an order shouted and then forget it before her hand touched the green curtain. Her mind was muddled by the lists of foods other people were demanding, by Nell saying, "Put up more cups, Molly," by Annis telling her, "The forks are on the second shelf." She had to pour coffee, endless coffee, keeping the cups always filled. She had to put out clean spoons and wipe the counter. Again, endlessly. She had a whole stack of napkins that she was supposed to fold when the counter became "slow." But it never did. Her chairs, those directly in front of her station, were always filled, and always with men. Some smelled of expensive cologne, others of human grime. They asked her name, where she was from. Molly didn't have time to smile, never mind answer.

When the breakfast rush ended at ten a.m., her body wanted to droop. Her feet ached as if she had walked from Streator to Chicago and back again. But Annis continued to assign tasks. Molly must refill the donut trays and pie stands from the breakfast shelf in the kitchen. She must bring out more cups and saucers from the shelves beside the washing sink. Only when the counter was restored to its pre-breakfast state was she was allowed to rest. "But don't go far," Annis warned.

Molly could only escape to the lounge. Gingerly, she removed her high-buttoned shoes. Her feet were swollen.

"Here." Violet was also taking a break. She brought Molly a piece of pear crumb cake and a tall glass of cool water. "I'm Violet, remember?"

"Yes," said Molly.

"Drink all the water you can," Violet advised. "I'm from Georgia. I know what it's like when you first come here. Being so thirsty makes you very tired!"

Molly took a sip, then found herself gulping. She wanted more water. Gallons more. But back behind the counter she had no spare moment in which to drink. The noon meal was even busier than breakfast. This time it wasn't just local men, but also two freight trains that stopped for coal, water, and crew breaks. Some of these train men smelled of smoke, others of the stale air of railway cars. Miraculously, Molly found that she was remembering orders. Only one order at a time, but still, an improvement. She discovered that Nell and Annis had been helping her all along, bringing food she had forgotten, refilling cups that she'd meant to refill.

So lunch was a tiny bit better than breakfast. Even so, by the time the lunch work slowed, Molly thought she might die of exhaustion right there in her clothes, leaving her shoes to walk the countless counter miles without her. "More milk, Molly," Annis called.

Milk meant the ice box. The ice box was in the kitchen. Molly grasped the pitcher and pushed aside the green curtain. She paused to let Violet pass by with a tray full of clean silver. Violet bumped open the swinging doors with her hip, and Molly caught a glimpse of the dining room and her sister. Colleen was brushing off a chair with a little whisk broom. Colleen was working energetically. She was talking to Faye and smiling.

How on earth could Colleen be *smiling*?

Molly filled her pitcher. She paused again at the busy spot. No more swings of the dining room doors. No more glimpses of Colleen.

The hours between two and five p.m. turned out to be the promised "slow" time. Only six or seven of the swivel chairs were occupied at any given moment, and Annis and Nell took care of those men. Molly was allowed to sit on the chair at the far end of the counter, near an outside door that Annis said was unlocked for nighttime customers. Molly's job, folding napkins, should have been easy. But after the exertions of breakfast and lunch, she found it took all of her strength just to pick up a square of cloth, fold it in half, fold it sideways, then set it down again.

At five o'clock the pace picked up, with local men who wanted early suppers. Then at six p.m., when Sissy and Jeanette came down the stairs, Molly was free. "Counter work is divided between day girls and night girls," Annis explained. "Eventually you and Colleen will take a night shift yourselves."

Molly couldn't imagine a night shift. She could scarcely imagine the next minutes to come. Her dulled mind didn't remember Jeanette, but she had no trouble recognizing Sissy. Sissy had arranged her hair so that her topknot reached just a little higher than before.

"So, say," Sissy said, with an unkind smile, "were you and your sister farm girls, factory girls, or rich girls?"

Molly's thoughts slid with sudden comfort back to the big house, the cooks and housemaids Colleen used to hire, the horses and carriage Papa owned before he became ill. "Rich, I suppose."

"Pampered," Sissy sniffed.

"Go on, now." Annis pushed the small of Molly's back in a friendly gesture. "You did just fine."

"Just fine." Molly repeated the words as she limped upstairs. She told them to her feet, after she carefully pulled off her shoes. She curled up on her bed with Jonathan's book beneath her head. She said the words to Papa's watch, now lying beside her stomach. "Just fine."

But her heart, and her every desire, was back in that big house. If only she were little again. If only she believed in magic. If only it would work, she would wind the watch backward so that Papa would still be alive. Mama too. Colleen would never have heard of the Harvey Girls. And Molly would be a rising eighth grader, wearing bright green hair ribbons to the first day of school.

→ ❈ ←

The next morning, Colleen shook Molly awake and then went back to bed herself. "Do fine again today, Molly," she said sleepily.

Molly had to put on her awful clothes and her too-tight shoes without encouragement. She had to eat her early breakfast with Miss Lambert, who sat with the counter girls, and whose presence limited everybody's conversation to pleasantries about the weather. The weather! Molly hadn't been outside for over a day.

"Yesterday I worked with your sister, Molly," Miss Lambert said, in that stiff way she had, untouchable through her elegance. "Today I'll be with you."

On this day of work, Molly learned the finer points: how to set the counter places exactly so, how to cut pies into four large pieces. "We give our customers as much, even more food than they want," Miss Lambert instructed.

Yesterday the men had joked with, even teased, the Harvey Girls. But today they were respectful. Today, the counter was almost hushed. And Molly discovered that she didn't feel quite so rushed. She felt stronger too. Miss Lambert, like Violet, understood the importance of water and allowed Molly to keep a glass for herself on the cup shelf just below the counter. "But only for these next two weeks, and only after our customers have everything they need."

"Our customers" were "a Harvey Girl's first concern." Molly's customers, on this day, got their food and beverages promptly, their every need swiftly satisfied. Today, Molly was two people, Molly and Miss Lambert. One half herself and one half perfection. Miss Lambert never spilled, splashed, or scattered food. Miss Lambert's hands stayed as clean as her lacy, beribboned apron. Unlike Molly, Miss Lambert never bumped into Annis or Nell. She stepped gracefully aside to make room for Annis to lift the coffee urn from its nook. "When Annis goes into the dining room, Molly," Miss Lambert said, "it will be your responsibility to keep the urn filled."

Dismayed, Molly watched Annis disappear behind the green curtain. Molly could no more lift that coffee urn than she could lift a house.

"You may fill it all at once, or pitcher by pitcher," Miss Lambert continued. "But the urn must never be empty."

The hours passed. Molly's mind emptied of everything but Harvey Girl concerns, and of those concerns she was full to bursting. She served food and cleared away. She kept the sugar bowls filled and the cream pitchers topped up. She remembered multiple orders too, as long as they weren't long or complicated. She – "Make an effort to be pleasant," Miss Lambert instructed. "Pleasant, but never familiar. Remember, you are a Harvey Girl." – smiled.

That evening, when she pulled herself up the stairs, she didn't feel quite as terrible as she had the night before. She washed her face and hands, then realized that she was hungry. Stocking-footed, she went back down to the kitchen for some supper.

She waited until the busy spot was clear. She grabbed a plate from the shelf set against the wall. She filled it with food from pans set over a row of spirit lamps.

"*Non, non!*" Gaston shouted at an assistant. His accent made his words sound as though they were disappearing into his nose. "You stir the sauce like *thees!*"

The busy spot opened for an instant, and Molly slid between Violet and the kitchen boy and into the lounge. Her feet begged her to sit down, but her eyes wanted to see something other than dishes and food, so she ate standing at the window. She had been inside the Harvey House for so long she had almost forgotten the existence of wind. But dust blew in little eddies down the unpaved street. A woman's skirt flattened against her legs. A man's hat flew up from his head.

There was only one woman on that street, but maybe eight or nine men. Molly had served hat-wearing men all day. The customers in peaked caps had smelled of railway cars. The shabby, porkpie-hatted men had smelled of coal. And the wide-brimmed felt hats belonged to the unwashed men, one of whom, she now saw, had a gun hanging at his hip.

Molly stood frozen, her fork halfway to her mouth. This was exactly what she had read about in *Billy the Kid and Company*: men and guns and bloody shootouts.

This gunman though, seemed to be battling nothing more ornery than the wind. He left the street to enter a clapboard building. *North State Laundry*. Within minutes he emerged carrying a brown-paper wrapped package.

Gunmen, it appeared, needed clean clothes too.

Molly finished eating her supper. She took her plate into the kitchen. The pace there was relaxed now, almost slow. Gaston threw up his hands and announced, "I have done my all. I can do no more today." He exchanged his tall chef's hat for a flat, round cap and left through the street-side door.

Molly was tempted to follow. But no, she wasn't ready to go out into that street. Not alone. Not yet. The only other place she could go was back upstairs. Annis and Nell had left their door open, so she peeked inside. Nell, or maybe Annis, had stuck an old valentine in the frame of the mirror. Molly didn't exactly snoop, but she turned the doorknobs to the other girls' rooms. She opened the doors just a crack.

In Sissy and Jeanette's room, it was obvious which bed was Sissy's. It was strewn with wads of false hair. Violet shared with Iona. Violet, or maybe it was Iona, owned a guitar. Next to them was the box room, where Faye had a cot, and where her fine blue silk hung high on the curtain rod.

Molly didn't have to be cautious about opening the balcony door. She stuck out her stockinged foot and immediately picked up a splinter from the bare boards. "Ow!" she said to the gust of wind that brushed her nose. She could have gone back to her room for shoes, but she wasn't willing to endure that pain unless she absolutely had to. So she only sniffed: dust, dryness, and something that was like, but wasn't quite, pine.

She didn't even consider opening Miss Lambert's doors.

Her own room, neat and prim from Colleen's efforts, looked hardly lived in. She hung her apron in the wardrobe. She loosened her corset so that she could sit cross-legged on her bed with Papa's watch on her lap. Then she put a piece of Colleen's note paper against the cover of *Billy the Kid and Company*, and began to write.

Dear Amy, I am now in Raton, New Mexico, where cowboys really walk around with guns on their hips. That should make Amy's eyes pop. Molly chewed on Colleen's pencil. *Please tell Jonathan I have not had the misfortune to meet a desperado.* She chewed on the pencil some more. What should she say next? "I miss you," sounded so feeble. How could she explain homesickness to a best friend who had never been more than ten miles from home?

The pencil was looking like a beaver stick. She heard Violet call to Nell. The hallway filled with the sounds of the dining room girls coming up to change clothes at the end of their shift. Their conversations suddenly stopped. Percussive noises, like firecrackers, punctured the silence.

Nell threw open the door to Molly's room. She charged to the window at the foot of Molly's bed, pushed through the curtains and crawled outside with practiced speed. "Gunshots," she said in passing.

Molly cowered, pressing her body against the wall. The other Harvey Girls were slamming the balcony door once, twice, many times. "Who's down there?" Annis asked, as clearly as if she were standing on the other side of Molly's window. Which, it turned out, she was. When Molly flicked the curtain aside, just an inch, she saw Annis's backside.

"Johnston," Nell replied. "Beneath the gas light."

"But of course," Violet sighed.

Then Molly heard a voice she knew as well as she knew her own. "Does he do this often?"

Molly opened the curtain another few inches. She tried to distinguish amongst the backs of other black skirts, the ties of other white aprons. She found Colleen's shoes.

"Only when he's drunk." Violet's soft voice was weighted with regret and displeasure.

"He's trying to shoot down Attorney Gleason's sign," Iona explained.

"He's a bad shot and a worse gambler." Nell ventured all the way over to the balcony railing.

Annis cleared some of Molly's view by joining Nell. Annis leaned so far over the railing, the bow of her sash rose higher than her head. "Go into the counter and get some coffee, Johnston," she called.

"Thank you, Miss Annis, I might should," a man's voice called back politely. And then he followed his words with two more sharp percussions.

"There goes the sign!" said Nell.

"He'll have to pay," Violet sighed.

Colleen brushed Molly's curtain open, uncovering Molly's face. "Why, Molly! There you are. Come out and join us."

"No," Molly said succinctly.

Colleen tsked mild annoyance, but let the curtain fall. Now Molly could hear the Harvey Girls settling into rocking chairs. The chairs squeaked. The girls' voices carried.

"What pies are at the counter tonight?" Iona asked, as if nothing at all had happened, as if they were just sitting there to feel the wind whoosh against their faces.

"Peach, with any luck," Annis said.

"It's peach pie that Johnston favors," Nell explained.

"My mother soaks her dried peaches in ginger water." Violet changed the subject.

Molly was amazed. She was *appalled*. What could she do but return to her cross-legged position? What conversation could she have, but with her true friend, so very far away? She stabbed her pencil on the paper. *You would not want to come here,* she wrote. *Nobody should want to come here. People get drunk and shoot down signs. And other people, people who know better, don't seem to care.*

Amy would never believe what Molly herself was having trouble believing. That Colleen, a Streator girl, *a Gerry daughter,* was right now exchanging recipes on the balcony while a criminal roamed the street below.

Chapter 4

"Look to New Mexico for incidents of the deepest, vilest crime." *Billy the Kid and Company*

Johnston did indeed favor peach pie. He ate peach pie for breakfast the next morning. It was Molly who had to serve him. He sat right in front of her, a thin, small, sun-wrinkled fellow. Diminutive compared to Annis who, Molly hoped, would knock him out cold with a syrup pitcher if he misbehaved. But Johnston showed no signs of misbehavior; Johnston was morose. He bent his face with its wreath of grizzled hair and beard down toward his third piece of peach pie, and he moped.

"You're a leatherhead, Johnston," said his neighbor, a man so smeared with engine grease that his fingers left prints on the dishes. "You know you ain't nothing without that mule."

"An' I was a-gonna go up to Elizabethtown," Johnston mourned. "Try for some gold."

Molly poured coffee for them both. There was something new about this morning, her third as a Harvey Girl. Something she couldn't quite identify. And then she realized what it was: she was following a conversation. Her hands were working just as hard and as fast as they should, but her ears had discovered that they could listen.

She poured tea for the one man who, unlike the others, was a gentleman. A man as finely dressed as … no, more finely dressed than Papa at his healthiest and most prosperous. This gentleman wore the most gorgeous waistcoat Molly had ever seen: bright purple, brilliantly embroidered with little Chinese houses. And he smelled of sandalwood cologne.

"I'm afraid you'll have to apply for re-entry to the coal mines, Johnston," the gentleman said. He had an accent, a real accent, nothing like the muddled way the other men spoke. His words were absolutely clear, beautifully enunciated. Maybe British? In appearance and speech he was as different from Johnston as an eagle was from a mud-spattered sparrow. But he talked to Johnston as though they were friends, as though they saw each other every day.

And they did. Or at least, they had seen each other for the last three days in a row. Molly had served them every time.

"How 'bout some sugar, Miss?" A different slurring of consonants and vowels. A different scent. This time, unwashed body odor. One of the cowboys tapped a bowl. Molly stared. She had served him before too. When she brought the sugar, she arched her neck so that she could see over the counter. His holster was empty. She scanned the hips of other cowboys. Every holster was empty. She rolled back onto her heels. Without guns, these men weren't much more than a source of stink: working-man stink, horse stink, old and damp leather stink.

"I cut out the dogie," that cowboy told another. "Had to bulldog the maverick."

What was he talking about?

She served other cowboys. She poured coffee for dozens of men. And all the time she listened. Most of what she heard made no sense at all. "So we built the pressure up to one hundred eighty pounds." "And then we cognisized the mine was salted." "I had to send a thirty on the line." Peaked caps addressed other peaked caps. Porkpie hats shared news with their own kind.

"It's good anthracite, shouldn't flame." With that incomprehensible statement, all but a few of the regulars left. The morning's freight train from Kansas City was coming in. Now Molly's chairs were filled with peak-hatted strangers who smelled of smoke and fire and the sharp iron-metal staleness of enclosed railroad cars. These men dropped foreign-sounding words. Las Vegas, Albuquerque, Tucson. The names of towns on the westward line.

Then they were gone. The breakfast rush was over. It was

time for the usual lull. Nell went for her break, so Molly was left alone with Annis. Johnston remained at the counter. He had stayed there all along, next to the gentleman and a few seats down from a man whose name, it turned out, was Jenkins. Jenkins spoke about things Molly could understand: his wife, his children, and the number of cattle being sent from the area ranches to eastern markets.

A new man – no, not entirely new – who wore a conductor's cap and brass buttons, slipped into a chair between Jenkins and Johnston. "Well, boys," he said, "here's the Denver news," and he spread a newspaper out on the counter.

Molly poured coffee and juice around it. The conductor wanted fried eggs and biscuits. She brought the food back and held it in the air until he noticed. He lowered the plate himself, covering up the *Rocky Mountain News* masthead.

The conductor, the gentleman, Jenkins, and Johnston all crowded over the paper.

"Genius Jim!" The gentleman shook his head in reproof at a headline.

"Left his mark at the Leadville job," the conductor told the others.

"They traced him all the way to Burlington, Iowa, it seems," Jenkins scanned.

"Read aloud," Johnston begged.

Jenkins obliged. "*Genius Jim and his Gang of Brains discovered – through what nefarious chicanery, we know not – that*

Mr. Cornelius Thornton, stagecoach driver, had hidden his passengers' valuables in the horse collars of his leading pair. Mrs. Molly Brown, cautious of the fate of her diamond drop earrings, had suggested the stratagem …"

Molly was supposed to be refilling the milk pitcher and bringing in more donuts. But she drifted closer, to eavesdrop. Her attention was on what she was hearing. Her hands were on their own. They poured coffee into the gentleman's tea cup.

"May I have another, clean cup, my dear?" he requested in his so-very-cultured voice.

Molly reached below the counter, felt no cups, then squatted to see. The cup shelf was empty. Her fault. She would have to fetch more. When she got back, the conductor was saying, with admiration, "Who but Genius Jim could have pulled that one off?"

"Who but?" the gentleman agreed. "Although the question that most burdens my mind is, *who is*? Who is this Genius Jim? What is his name when he is at home? Where is that home?"

"Ain't nobody knows," said Johnston.

"Exactly," the gentleman replied. "By the descriptions we hear he could be anybody, or everybody. He could be you, Johnston, with an ideal disguise, a prospector just down from Colorado."

Johnston guffawed, "Me?"

"Or an even better disguise," the gentleman continued. "What individual could be more innocent than a married man with a compliant wife and three promising children? A leading citizen of one of this nation's many small towns. A freight agent, for example, who knows all the transportation lines in the West. Someone like Jenkins here."

"Nonsense," Jenkins sputtered.

"But if I were Genius Jim," the gentleman said thoughtfully, "I would choose to be a conductor, traveling daily from one spot to the other, knowing which trains carry the wealthiest passengers."

All of the men, and Molly, stared at the potentially guilty conductor.

"And if I were Genius Jim," the conductor returned, "I would talk with a fancy accent and pretend to be a rich foreigner. A dude turned rancher, for example. Here's my question to you, Gravity. Did you really bring all that money over from England? Or did you rob it from my trains?"

The four men laughed.

"You can take your break now, Molly," Annis said, and Molly's attention switched like a train on a track back to the Harvey World, to her job, to an awareness of her own hungry stomach.

She went into the kitchen to fill a plate with dinner food just set out on the long kitchen shelf. "*Thees* tool is impossible!" the chef shouted, and Molly thought, *Genius Jim could be French.*

Inside or outside, no place in this whole town was guaranteed to be safe. So she opened the kitchen door and stepped out onto the porch. She gulped in what felt like the freshest air she had ever known. What a relief to no longer smell food, or men, or sandalwood cologne! Instead, she inhaled a dry, dry dust – what would have been drought dust in Illinois. But here, the dust smelled and tasted wonderful.

Her lungs full to bursting, she un-narrowed her eyes and blinked against the New Mexico sunlight. Nobody, but nobody, was out on the street. She examined the board floor on which she was standing, the posts that held up the balcony above, the steps down to the dirt. Everything was so very bright, so unnaturally clear. Everything had such sharp edges, such dark shadows.

She set her plate down on the top step, sat beside it, and began to eat. A miner walked by. Miners! Another perfect disguise for a master thief and train robber.

The kitchen boy came out from the Harvey House behind her. The New Mexico sun highlighted him, just as it did everything else. His hair was black, his face bronzed. He was shorter than Molly, but wiry and strong. His arms were red and chapped all the way to the elbows. He tossed water onto a low and sorry rose bush that was trying to grow against the porch.

He was much too young to be Genius Jim. Molly tried to guess his age. Probably a few years older than her. Fifteen? He had just the hint of a beginning beard. "That water's a little dark," she said, by way of starting a conversation.

"Potato water," the boy replied. He had an accent too,

but not British or muddled American. He stood with the pot hanging from his hand. He stretched his head and neck up, turning his face to the sun. He seemed to drink in the light, as if it was that, not air, that his body needed.

"For a rose?" Molly asked.

"Gaston's rose," the boy replied.

"How long have you worked here?" Molly queried.

The boy didn't answer. He simply brought his face down from the sun and went back inside.

Soon Molly would have to return to work too. She picked up her fork again. Today's chicken was sauced with rosemary and thyme and slices of something that wasn't exactly mushrooms. This Harvey House food was the best she had ever eaten. Here was another mystery, something else that didn't make sense. How could such excellent food exist in a land of the vilest crimes?

→ ⚜ ←

Molly had Thursday off, which was a pleasant surprise. Miss Lambert said she would have a day off every ten days or so, and Molly was wearily grateful. On Thursday, she rose late. She shared breakfast with Colleen. Colleen started work, and Molly went outside to stand on the Harvey House porch. She drank in the air – still dry, but less dusty today – and considered her options.

Colleen had assigned her both a task and a rule of conduct. Molly was to buy a new pair of shoes; Molly was to comport herself as an adult at all times.

She stepped down into the street. Dust billowed, clinging to the hem of Mama's skirt. Molly grasped the cloth around her hips and hitched upward.

Because she was looking down, she at first didn't notice a fat cowboy passing by. "Hello, Miss Molly," he said, tipping his hat.

Another man, an engineer, also greeted her. "Good morning, Miss Molly." Molly knew him by name. He was called Soffit, and he sometimes came to the counter.

Attorney Gleason emerged from his office across the street. He was one of Molly's regulars. He examined his brand new sign and called out, "What do you think, Miss Molly?"

Miss Molly. They all knew her as Miss Molly. Still holding up her skirt, she crossed over, imprinting the soles of her high-buttoned shoes in the dust. At the boardwalk, she let her skirt drop. "It's very nice," she complimented, even though the sign was only a painted piece of wood, nothing special.

"It will do until Johnston shoots it out again," Attorney Gleason said, satisfied.

Papa's sign had been five feet tall and eight feet in width, with green four-leaf clovers as the background and three of the letters, G, R, and Y, framing the faces of leprechauns. Papa's sign had been magnificent.

Molly continued down the boardwalk, judging other merchants' attempts to advertise themselves. Most of the signs were as simple and as incorrect as it was possible to be:

misspelled words burned into gray-weathered doors or painted onto filthy windows. Even the butcher's window, *BUCHR*, was dotted with flies. Disgusting!

Gaston's beef arrived in a refrigerator car from Kansas City, already cut and clean and wholesome. Molly hitched up her skirt again, even though the boardwalk was guilty only of tobacco spit. She walked on.

Next door to the North State Laundry was Bloutcher's Boots and Shoes. Mr. Bloutcher was one of the few who had bothered to paint his storefront, but to little avail. The paint had been applied over so much dirt and grime, it was bumpy in some places and peeling in others. When Molly pushed on the door, gobby paint jammed against gobby paint. Molly shoved. The paint gave, shreds falling to the threshold. A little bell tingled above her head, and a man appeared from a back room.

"Why, Miss Molly!" he said cheerfully.

Here was someone else who knew her – or thought he did. "I need shoes, please." She extended her foot in its dainty Streator purchase, once bright-white and shiny-black leather, now mostly beige-gray from Raton dust.

"What's your pleasure?" Mr. Bloutcher waved his hand past miners' boots, cowboys' boots, the less sturdy shoes worn by Englishmen and attorneys, even some men's dancing slippers, to settle on the one pair that was faintly feminine. Black lace-ups with low heels. Harvey Girl shoes.

Molly hated them on sight. "Do you have anything else?"

she asked.

"We can order," Mr. Bloutcher said agreeably. "I have a catalog."

But Molly needed new shoes right away. Colleen had insisted. Molly's feet and legs and spine all insisted too. Only Molly's taste and sense of style rebelled. But taste and style were no match for Mr. Bloutcher, who got Molly into a chair, made her take off her shoes, then made her stand again so that he could measure her feet. "Excellent!" he exclaimed. "I'll be right back."

He returned with a pair that he slid over Molly's stockings. While he laced, he chatted. "I saw Miss Colleen in the dining room when I took dinner there a few days ago. I don't often eat at the Harvey House. Mostly, Mrs. Bloutcher insists I come home. No mistaking the two of you are related. How do these fit?"

They fit perfectly. They were a thousand times more comfortable than Molly's button-ups. "Fine," she regretted.

"Wear them in good health!"

Molly didn't want to be seen in them. Not yet. Not on a day when she wasn't exactly a Harvey Girl. Not when she was wearing Mama's dress. "Will you wrap them?"

Outside Mr. Bloutcher's shop, she continued north. She passed by a saddlery and a blacksmith. The railroad tracks on the other side of the street divided, then divided again. Raton's main street, called Front Street, ended at a curved building, a huge half-circle. It wasn't so much a building as a barn, with stalls for a dozen locomotives and a giant lazy Susan out front. Right now, one of the locomotives was stopped on the lazy Susan. Half a dozen men, wielding paintbrushes dripping a bright canary yellow, swarmed all over it.

"Little Buttercup." Engineer Soffit yelled to Molly. He pointed at the locomotive.

She waved in response.

That was the end of Front Street. Molly should turn around and go back. But the very last storefront, the one right before the locomotive barn, was something that didn't exist in Streator. In Streator, the Women's Christian Temperance Union was active and strong. In Raton, the citizenry allowed a saloon.

Molly paused. This sign was another poor attempt. No words, just a painted daisy. Molly spied toward the Harvey House. Nobody was watching her. She glanced sidewise at the double swinging doors. Tall as she was, she couldn't see over them. She stooped to adjust her shoe – which needed no adjusting – so that she could crane her neck and peer beneath the doors. She saw nothing but darkness. She caught a whiff of old tobacco. She listened for voices, but she heard only a train whistle from the distance and then Mr. Thomas's gong.

"Good morning, Miss Molly."

She stood up immediately, flushed and guilty. But the man who had greeted her just walked on.

So, she did too. Past the blacksmith, the saddlery, Bloutcher's Boots and Shoes, North State Laundry, the butcher's. Raton had no milliner's, no candy store, no shops to attract women or girls. Except for maybe Dacy's Mercantile. Molly pushed that door open and was hit by a wave of homesickness so powerful she gasped. It was the smells. Pickles and crackers and soap and packaged seeds. She closed her eyes and was immediately back home, breathing in the special mustiness that belonged to a store so crammed with merchandise it could never be adequately dusted. Papa was busy behind the sales counter, and in a moment he would call out, "Molly-girl!"

"Miss Molly?"

She opened her eyes. The man from the saloon was holding out a hand as if to keep her from fainting. Two of his fingers were missing. "Are you all right? I'm Chad Bellamy, brakeman on the Little Buttercup."

"I'm fine, thank you." Molly forced herself to look away from his stumps. How did a person lose *fingers*? He left through the door Molly had just entered, his good hand holding a can of yellow paint.

Papa sold paint too. But there the similarity ended. Papa didn't stock these strangely-shaped tools. Papa would never have offered such roughly-woven blankets. Papa sold only the finest of items. At Papa's store, a person could find kid gloves, French lace, and dozens of shades of silk ribbon. Dacy's Mercantile only offered thick leather leggings, heavy iron spurs, and big bottles of a solution that promised to strip engine grease off of hands and out of clothes. Molly had to search high and low for cloth, and then her choice was limited to black or dark blue wool. She had to search even harder before she found ribbon – cheap cotton ribbon in only three colors.

She picked up the bolt of black wool. She chose the spool of red ribbon. "I'd like a yard of each, please," she told the man at the cash register.

"Welcome, Miss Molly. I've sat at your sister's table, twice."

Another person who thought he knew Molly. But, like all the other residents of this town, he only knew her clothes: a Harvey Girl's uniform and a grown-up lady's dress. Molly was suddenly, indescribably lonely. She paid for her purchases with what was left of the money Colleen had given to her. She turned to leave and found herself face-to-face with the Harvey House kitchen girl. "Hello!" she said, almost desperately. It would be so good to talk with someone who was her *real* age.

The kitchen girl raised her eyebrows.

"Is today your day off too?" Molly asked. "Are you going right back?"

The girl cut Molly short. "Josiah said you talked," she remarked, in the most unfriendly tone imaginable. "Do you know no better?"

Molly stood hurt. The girl walked around her coldly, avoidingly, to buy a packet of washing powder from Mr. Dacy.

Mr. Dacy served the girl with obvious reluctance. She wasn't quite out of the store when he declared, loud enough for her to hear, "Greasers and half-breeds, they're all the same.

You'd do best to stay away from them, Miss Molly."

Molly was horribly humiliated. She was dreadfully embarrassed. She waited only long enough to be certain that the girl was well away from Dacy's Mercantile before she darted out. She ran up the Harvey House porch, intending to thrust open the door, speed up the stairs, and then hide herself in her bedroom.

But she entered a scene of such chaos she had to slow down. The busy spot was jammed with dining room girls wheeling in cart after cart, bringing in tray after tray. Gaston, instead of directing the usually smooth clockwork of activity, leaned against a wall, fanning himself with his hat, silent in word if not in gesture. He was exhausted. His assistant cooks scrubbed the table and the stove. The kitchen boy stood surrounded by dirty dishes, some even on the floor at his feet. He was emptying the package of washing powder into the sink. The kitchen girl stood beside him, scraping leavings from a big meat roaster into the waste pail.

"You!" Only Sissy took the time to say anything to Molly. "Where have *you* been?"

"Shopping." Molly held out her packages in proof.

"It was a Full House," Sissy scolded. "A full train. When it's Full House, everybody works. Even day off girls. Even the night shift. *I* should be sleeping."

"I didn't know," Molly pleaded.

"You don't know how to *work*," Sissy emphasized, "*You've* never been in a factory. Rich girls!" Somehow, she could flounce even when carrying a tray half as large as she was. She flounced away, leaving Molly scorned. Again.

No need now to rush or to hurry. Everybody who disliked Molly, everybody who thought they knew her, had seen her long enough. She crept up the stairs toward the refuge of her room. She would get into bed and hide beneath the blankets. She would stay there for the rest of her life.

$$\rightarrow \text{⊰⊱} \leftarrow$$

Unlike Sissy, Miss Lambert didn't think Molly incapable. Quite the reverse. Early the next morning, Miss Lambert deemed that Molly had advanced from doing "fine" to being an "adequate" waitress. She even promoted Molly, in a way. Annis was sent to her new post in the dining room. From now on, Molly and Nell would divide the counter tasks between them.

Molly scarcely had time to get used to this idea before Mr. Thomas unlocked the door, and the morning regulars poured in. Molly's panic – immense – was overcome by the even more overwhelming demands of her customers. She had no time to think; she could only move in her now well-practiced routine. She automatically called for Gravity's tea when she heard his voice, before she even saw him take off his hat. She put a glass of orange juice before Engineer Soffit's favorite chair without being asked.

She called out four orders at once and didn't forget to whom the food belonged when it appeared on the shelf.

"You're doing famously!" Nell whispered, squeezing Molly's shoulder when they met at the coffee urn.

Molly should have been pleased, but she wasn't. She was no more pleased by Nell's compliment of "famously" than she had been by Miss Lambert's assessment of "adequate." Overnight, Molly had made up her mind. She was going to find a way to stop being a Harvey Girl, come hail or high water.

The end of her shift finally arrived. Violet and Iona took over. Molly was free to do whatever she wanted. Which wasn't much, within the limits of Harvey Girl life. She stalked through the green curtain, keeping her nose turned away from the kitchen girl who, she now knew from hasty glances while fetching coffee, mostly spent her time following Gaston around.

"Susana!" Gaston called, and the girl bent to pick up a saucepan lid that he had knocked to the floor.

Molly deigned to watch no longer. She snatched some supper from the long shelf and ate it all by herself in the lounge. She was supposed to return her dishes to the washing sink, but she wasn't going to go anywhere near that kitchen boy. So she sinned, mightily, leaving her dirty dishes on the table for Nell to clear.

Upstairs in her room, she sat on the only chair that the Harvey establishment had thought to provide, and commenced on an absolutely non-Harvey-girl task. Squinting and biting her tongue, she carefully picked away at the side seam threads in her uniform skirts, managing to only snip the skirts themselves once or twice. Maybe three or four times. But not enough that anyone, especially not Colleen, would ever notice. Then she set about cutting pocket shapes from Mr. Dacy's black fabric. This was easier.

"What? You, Molly, sewing?" Two hours must have passed, because Colleen was upstairs too. She hardly looked at what Molly was doing. She showed no interest at all. Instead, she changed her clothes swiftly, calling, "I'll be right there!" to someone out in the hall. She had left their door partially open.

The other Harvey Girls were gathering. Molly could hear them. "*Oooooo!*" Nell exclaimed. "Was this your mother's lace?"

"I brought it with me," Faye said. "I had hopes."

"*Ooo!*" Nell said again.

"This petticoat might be too long for you, Faye," Colleen called. And without asking Molly's permission, she pulled one of Mama's petticoats from the wardrobe. "But I can shorten it." With absolutely no consideration for Molly, without the slightest concern for Molly's comfort or recognition of Molly's need, she tugged the chair out from under Molly's bottom. She carried the chair through the doorway. "Stand up here, Faye, so I can measure."

Molly was left standing, with fabric and thread dangling from her hands. Absolutely, utterly, totally offended, she went to the door. They were all there – with the exception of Violet and Iona, who were working the night shift, and Sissy, whom nobody liked.

"This is what Paul said about marriage." Jeanette began reading aloud from a Bible.

The other girls paid Jeanette scant attention. They clustered around Faye, who was dressed as a bride. Well, almost as a bride. Faye still wore her work stockings and shoes. She climbed up on Molly's chair with help from Annis, and the girls all *Ooo'd* with Nell.

Molly narrowed her eyes. She wouldn't have *Ooo'd*, even if she had been invited. Faye's wedding gown was at least twenty years out of fashion.

Colleen knelt at Faye's feet, so that her gaze was in line with Faye's ankles. "I'll have to shorten the petticoat about three inches," Colleen declared. "Bring me the pins, Molly."

Molly turned, helpless against what she now recognized as a lifelong habit of sisterly servitude. She fetched and provided the pins.

"I wish the neckline was just a bit lower." Faye touched her bosom.

"I can do that too. Scissors, Molly."

Molly slapped the scissors into Colleen's hand.

Then she stepped back into their room and slammed the door. It wasn't much of a protest, but it should serve to remind Colleen that Molly wasn't just a seamstress's maid, but existed as a person in her own right.

She returned to her own sewing. Her hands weren't as deft as Colleen's, but they were "adequate." Her fingers pushed and pulled. She stitched the pocket shapes into pockets.

She attached them, one into each skirt. She slid her new red ribbon through the hoop on Mr. Latterly's four-leaf clover.

And the next morning, she was a rebel. A covert, jewelry-wearing rebel. Papa's watch was a satisfying clunk against her thigh whenever she moved. The bright red ribbon, layered under Harvey black and white, glowed defiantly against her throat. Molly was connected to her past. She was talismaned against the future. As such, she served Johnston's pie. She poured Gravity's tea. And all the while, from deep inside, she blazed out resentment at the counter, the food, her customers.

None of whom seemed to notice.

"That Stanley's a lucky fellow," Johnston sighed.

"He's New Jersey. She's New Jersey." Jenkins shrugged. "A reasonable match."

"I'm taking them. Little Buttercup," said Engineer Soffit. "I'm gonna toot them all the way to Newton."

"Women like to live near their families," Gravity observed. "It was Miss Faye's wish to return East."

That sentence rapped gently against Molly's mind. Then it knocked, harder. She took note of it. Abruptly, she surfaced from her ire.

"I got me a bugle," said a man whose hair dripped coal dust onto the counter.

"We'll give them a booming send-off," said Jenkins. "I had Armstrong telegraph Newark. When those two disembark in New Jersey, every train on every track is going to blast its horn."

"Ain't that lovely." Rough and grizzled Johnston was soft with sentiment.

Molly felt her own *Ooo* welling in her throat – an *Ooo* of inspiration, an *Ooo* of hope. She served donuts and cinnamon buns. She spooned coffee-browned lumps out of sugar bowls. She called out orders, "Two meat loaf sandwiches, pork chop with gravy, mashed potatoes." And all the while, her mind sparked. Faye! Faye was going home.

→ ⚜ ←

Faye's wedding was on Saturday, scheduled around the Atchison, Topeka and Santa Fe Railway timetable. In between trains, the dining room became both chapel and reception hall. Faye wore her Colleen-remodeled white satin and her mother's lace veil. The groom wore traditional black.

Molly wore Mama's dove gray, with the four-leaf clover prominently displayed. Other people smiled and wept. Molly assessed. Like a cowboy buying a new horse, like an engineer examining someone else's locomotive, she studied Stanley's face, his height, the moneyed gloss of his top hat.

"I do," said Faye.

"I do," said Stanley.

The other guests clapped their congratulations. Mr. Thomas offered a toast. People gathered around the new couple, waiting for a kiss or a hand clasp. But Molly didn't go forward. Instead, she bored her index finger into the groove that centered the clover. She switched her analysis from

Stanley to his friends.

A locomotive fireman – the one whose hair usually sprinkled black dust – sped toward Colleen. "Miss Colleen," he offered her glass of punch.

"Thank you." Colleen accepted it, but she didn't flirt. She never flirted anymore, not like she used to, way back in Streator, before Papa's illness. Back then, she'd worn pretty clothes. Of course now she mostly couldn't, because of having to wear the uniform. But still, even at this wedding, her dress was all black. Black wasn't Colleen's best color. Colleen should be wearing green. Green would help her attract …

"Now, I wouldna wanna go home," the engine fireman was saying. "Ain't nowhere to live but the West!"

… not this man.

One by one, Molly dismissed or selected from amongst Stanley's remaining friends. Gravity was too old. Jenkins was married. Ditto Attorney Gleason. Engineer Soffit and Armstrong, the day telegrapher, held promise.

Molly assessed them all, she weighed them in her hand. Inspiration had given her a goal, and that goal was now a plan. Molly was going to find her sister a husband.

Chapter 5

"Back East the girls chant 'Butcher, baker, candlestick maker.' Out West they cry 'Rancher, miner, railroad man.'" *The Atchison, Topeka and Santa Fe Railway Guidebook*

Engineer Soffit had been raised in Colorado City from the age of six. He loved, loved, *loved* the Rocky Mountains. He wasn't right for Colleen, not at all.

Telegrapher Armstrong spent the slow hours at his machine sending out a constant stream of *22-22-22*s.

Molly discovered all this by asking questions while working at the counter. Of course she couldn't *really* ask questions, not as she was aching to do. One of Miss Lambert's dictums was that Harvey Girls must not enter into conversations with customers. But Molly could elicit information in the same way that Nell did, by murmuring two or three words now and then while serving sandwiches.

"Twenty-two?" she said, her voice inflecting upward at the end to indicate that she didn't know what those numbers meant.

Soffit was happy to supply the answer, both to oblige Molly and to tease Armstrong. "Love and kisses, Love and kisses," he crooned. "Old Armstrong here's crazy for a little Hoosier gal."

Cross out Armstrong.

She moved down the counter to a trio of cowboys, pungent with their distinctive odor. Surely Colleen would never be interested in a man who *smelled*. But still, "Cowboy back East?" she posited.

The cowboys fell silent, trying to understand. They, like everybody else, knew that Molly was a beginner at Nell's short-talk. They waited until she could find another two or three words to express what she wanted.

"Cowboy go home?"

That was how she learned that a real cowboy was as likely to ride with his saddle upside down and inside out as to wish to return his hand to a plow.

Just as well. That stench would have proved too much to live with anyway.

She spent the rest of the day interviewing and then rejecting miners: pitmen, mining engineers and prospectors.

Miners complained constantly of poverty, "too broke to ride a train even if I was tied to the cowcatcher," while non-stop dreaming of that one strike that would make them "richer than Old Man Roosevelt!"

Miners weren't reliable, home-loving, Streator types.

Shopkeepers were. Or should be. Colleen, with her experience, would make an excellent shopkeeper's wife. But few of the store owners in Raton sold items that would be of interest to civilized people. And those few who did, like the butcher, well, Streator already had a *clean* butcher, an excellent baker, an experienced launderer.

So Molly was forced back to the railroad men. Another day of listening and questioning, and all she learned was that they were an unfortunately adventurous group whose minds were always traveling west. She sought amongst them for a compliant, Stanley-like fellow, but the closest she came was that soot-laden fireman, McCarty, whose only sign of possible compliance was his interest in Colleen.

If Molly could only find a Stanley-like streak somewhere behind McCarty's coal dust! If she could only inspire him to dote on, to worship, to love Colleen more than he did the West! If she could only re-orient his focus away from his locomotive firebox, and turn it eastward.

She tried to figure out ways to do exactly that while cutting him extra-large pieces of pie.

And then, later that week, just before one of her irregular days off, Mr. Latterly blew back into Molly's life.

He arrived on the 3:48 train from Arizona, and at first Molly didn't recognize him. She saw only another passenger amongst the many at the counter, another man in a gentleman's suit politely standing aside so that the ladies, in their huge, plumed hats, could sit first. And then it was his turn to take a chair.

"So, we meet again!" he said cheerfully.

Molly ignored the familiarity with a Miss Lambert-approved, "Coffee, Sir?"

"Have you forgotten, Miss Molly?"

He knew her name, but she didn't know his. That, of course, wasn't unusual here in Raton. But something about this man pulled at her memory. Not his features, so ordinary. Or his expression, so bland. It was his eyes, blinking behind their spectacles, and the way that her mind suddenly filled with tedious fact after tedious fact. "Mr. Latterly!"

Miss Lambert passed by, and Molly immediately returned to Harvey Girl demure. And code. "Owe money," she recalled.

"Eight cents," he clarified. "Will I find your sister in the dining room?"

And Molly remembered something else about Mr. Latterly. He had been sweet on Colleen. Hope rose, choking her voice. "Going home?" she squeaked.

Mr. Latterly took a sip of his coffee. "Chicago," he confirmed.

Molly could hardly breathe for excitement. "Colleen! Dining room!"

After her shift ended, she crouched halfway up the stairs while the dining room girls came in and out through the swinging door. Her glimpses of Mr. Latterly made him look like a man in a flip book – smiling up at Colleen, then eating, then smiling, then eating. Molly's mind fizzed with possibilities.

"Whatever are you doing, Molly?" Annis asked, pausing with two trays of dessert plates. Sissy darted, not having to bend, beneath Annis's upheld arms.

"Praying," Molly said honestly.

The doors stopped swinging with the end of the supper service. In another fifteen or twenty minutes, Colleen would be finished with her clearing-up tasks. In another fifteen minutes Molly could begin convincing her sister.

Meanwhile, down below, the kitchen also prepared itself for night. One cook blackened the stove. Another took clean pots and hung them on a rack. Susana gathered dirty rags and towels to put in a laundry sack. "Leave!" Gaston imperiously ordered the cooks. "Stay!" he told Susana and Josiah. "We will have dictation."

Molly, half-hidden, watched through the balustrade as Susana removed pencil and paper from a drawer in the kitchen table. Josiah continued to wash dishes. "Duck," Gaston pronounced.

Susana wrote, and Josiah spelled out loud. "D-U-K."

"No, no, Josiah," Gaston corrected. "Remember, in the English, every word is crazy." He continued, "Olives."

It was the strangest spelling lesson Molly had ever witnessed. In truth, it was a shopping list. And while Gaston was the teacher, his spelling was almost as bad as Josiah's. He thought "sugar" was spelled with an "er" not an "ar."

But then the dining room doors opened for the last time, and the Harvey Girls poured through, and – finally! – Molly could give Colleen the very sweaty nickel and three pennies she had been clutching for two long hours. "These-are-for-Mr. Latterly," she said, all in a rush. "Won't you take them to him? He has been so very kind to me, Colleen. And I know he wants to talk to you."

"Money?" Colleen flattened herself against the wall so the other girls could squeeze by.

"He even let me buy on credit!"

"Then you should pay him yourself." Colleen handed the coins back. "You can do it tomorrow. He's staying over so that he can take me driving on Thursday."

> ✦ ⋙✦⋘ ✦

The next morning, Molly awakened with a plan clutched in her mind like yesterday's coins in her fist. She bounded out of bed. Today was *her* day off! She dressed up in Mama's dove gray. She squeezed on her high-buttoned shoes. She skipped breakfast to rush out to the street. And there he was, carrying his black case, approaching the spot where Sheriff Armbruster (married) was pasting up a poster on the wall of the North State Laundry.

Molly scooped up her skirt. She darted. "Hello!" she panted.

"Why, Miss Molly!" The sheriff turned, his brush dripping paste in an arc.

Molly blazed a smile at Mr. Latterly.

"Good morning to you." He touched his free hand to his hat.

The sheriff smiled benignly on them both. "Already know each other, I see."

"I believe I am one of the Gerry sisters' first Western acquaintances," said Mr. Latterly. "Is that not so?"

"He is!" Molly certified.

"Salesman?" The sheriff pointed his brush at Mr. Latterly's case.

"Eyeglasses," Mr. Latterly explained. He peered through his own spectacles at the sheriff's sign.

"Genius Jim," Sheriff Armbruster explained. "Heisted a shipment of gold worth upwards of *ten thousand dollars*." The sheriff enunciated the amount as if he could hardly believe the existence of so much money. "Down in Douglas."

Beneath the big word, *WANTED*, there was a sketch of a face with nothing but sinister eyes. Everything below the nose was concealed by a blank triangle, probably a kerchief. "May I have one of your posters?" Molly begged. "For a friend?"

"Why, sure," Sheriff Armbruster obliged.

Molly rolled the flimsy newsprint into a scroll. Then she waited for the men to finish discussing all the details of the heist. "He's called *Genius* for good reason." Mr. Latterly, at long last, concluded the conversation. He must have sensed that Molly was following him, because he very politely held open the mercantile door for her.

This time, when Molly entered, she inhaled the promise of a return to her old life.

"I have the finest spectacles." Mr. Latterly went right up to the cash register to open his case for Mr. Dacy.

For thirteen years, Molly had heard sales pitches for spectacles, hair oil, tooth powder, shovels, and vegetable seeds. Once, back in Illinois, a salesman opened a tin of peaches from South Carolina to prove that his were the very best. Papa had given Molly and Amy the whole can. They ate it all, sweet syrup running down their chins. Papa had laughed, saying, "No need to prove that those are tasty!" and he bought a dozen cases.

"No need for you to worry, Miss!"

Molly started, then discovered that she was blindly staring into one of Mr. Dacy's glass display boxes. On the other side of her reflection – a thirteen-year-old's face, an eighteen-year-old's upswept and knotted hair – were knives. Knives of different sizes, shapes and handles. Knives for cowboys, hunters, prospectors, and railroad men. Deadly knives.

"You don't need protection here, Miss Molly," Mr. Dacy assured her. "You're safe in Raton. This town is patrolled by the Raton Vigilantes." He pointed to his chest. "R.V."

"The courage and skill of the Raton Vigilantes is well known throughout the territories," Mr. Latterly prudently complimented.

"We do our best." Mr. Dacy was appropriately gratified, so

Mr. Latterly was appropriately rewarded. "I'll take a dozen of those specs for far, and a dozen for near. And I thank you, sir, for these." Mr. Dacy pointed to the pair newly perched on top of his head. "Didn't know I could see print so well!"

This time, when Mr. Latterly opened the door, he seemed to expect that Molly would fall into step beside him. So she did. She was pleased to no longer be stalking. She was almost "walking," like Nell did with her railroader escort. The experience was novel. Mr. Latterly paused when Molly had to walk around spots of tobacco juice. He touched her elbow when a wagon careened too close to the boardwalk. Molly found the attention most enjoyable.

"Have you seen Second and Third Streets yet?" she invited, in a gentlewomanly manner.

Mr. Latterly had not. They turned right. Mr. Latterly began listing information, "Notice that mahogany front door with leaded glass. I expect that house, and the one next door, were freighted from Chicago."

Molly took a deep breath. She exhaled out an interruption. "My sister is so looking forward to driving with you tomorrow."

Mr. Latterly, halted mid-sentence, was blank-faced for a moment. Then he appeared as gratified as Mr. Dacy. "Really?"

"Colleen enjoyed our train ride together so very much," Molly said, which was maybe something of an exaggeration. "Colleen has spoken of you often since we last met," which was an outright lie. "She says you are the one gentleman with whom she feels comfortable out here in the West," which was enough to send Molly to confession for the rest of her life, but had the effect she was hoping for.

When Mr. Latterly brightened, even the eyeglasses on his nose seemed to sparkle. "Really!"

"Yes." Molly tried to curb, to stamp down, to squelch her eagerness. "As you know, we had to become Harvey Girls when our father died. But I know that Colleen would be much happier married, living in a home of her own. With me, of course."

Mr. Latterly stared at her. Then he turned his head to stare at the house with the leaded glass door. "I have sometimes thought that it would be beneficial to settle down," he remarked, but mostly to himself. "It often profits a salesman to have a home, a base, a special community in which he is known and respected."

And Molly lost all restraint. "What Colleen wants is to return to Illinois! What Colleen wants is to live in Streator again!"

"That small town near Chicago? No, not so near. Eighty miles." Mr. Latterly had to get the distance exactly right.

"Yes, yes!"

"Not inconvenient." Mr. Latterly's sparkle had dulled. No, not dulled, but become a steady, hopeful gleam. "She really likes me?" His voice was almost shy.

"Yes!" Molly willingly doomed herself to an eternity of penance – as long as she got a lifetime in Streator in return.

Mr. Latterly seemed only to want to think now. So this time, Molly escorted him. It was her grab to his arm that prevented him from stepping in front of Johnston's mule. Tenderly, she steered him back to the Harvey House. She inserted him into a chair at one of Colleen's tables. She watched over him as long as she could, until Miss Lambert ordered her out of the dining room.

Then she flew upstairs. Once behind her closed door, she unrolled the poster of Genius Jim. She wrote on its back in large, triumphant letters, *Dear Jonathan, tell Amy that I'm coming home.*

> ⚜ <

On Thursday, Molly said goodbye to everything, even though Colleen and Mr. Latterly weren't married yet, even though they were only gone for the day. Molly was too happy to wait. She thought *Goodbye!* to the coffee urn and the green curtain and the shelf where the food appeared. She served Gravity's tea with a goodbye flourish.

The breakfast regulars were busy discussing the heisted gold, but Molly didn't care. What did Genius Jim matter to her life? She was returning East.

"More donuts?" A cowboy she didn't know gazed at her as if he hadn't seen a female in a very long time.

Molly smiled with professional distance. *Goodbye!* In a matter of days, well, maybe a week, well, probably two weeks, she would no longer be a Harvey Girl. In the meantime, she was willing. She served donuts.

Too busy to refill the urn herself, she shouted "Coffee!" through the curtain. Sometimes, when the counter was exceptionally rushed, she had to do this. Now she danced from task to task, taking four orders from four customers, pouring milk, cutting up a fresh coconut pie. "Two steak and cheese sandwiches wrapped in paper, with pickles," she shouted. She stuck her head and shoulders through the green curtain just in time to take the coffee from Josiah, who was also bringing four breakfasts and two early lunches. She elbowed the curtain aside so he could set his plates and bundles on the shelf; he stepped forward. At that same moment the door to the dining room swung open with Sissy backing into the busy spot, pulling a cart covered with dirty dishes.

Molly saw it all: Josiah still on one foot; Sissy's black-clad bottom hitting his standing leg; Josiah wavering, his tower of food shifting in the air like plates on a clown's balancing stick.

"Oh!" he moaned.

And the tower came tumbling down. Pancakes, potatoes, tomatoes. Eggs fried, scrambled, and boiled. Two sandwiches with their paper wrappings tearing to spill out four pickles. Plates large and small. Not the best china, which was reserved for the dining room, but the thick and heavy china the kitchen used for counter food. The kind of china that, when it broke, left daggers to fall on.

Which Sissy did. She slipped on some tomatoes or

potatoes and fell half on Josiah and half on a broken plate. She screamed. Molly reached out a hand to help, but Sissy slapped it away.

"I'm hurt!" Sissy wailed.

Gaston came running. "Get up right now," he scolded Josiah, which was impossible since Josiah was pinned by Sissy's weight.

Miss Lambert rushed down the stairs. "What happened?"

Mr. Thomas flung open the swinging door from the dining room, hitting Sissy's cart and dislodging six more plates – fine china, this time – which shattered into tiny fragments. "Quell this row!" Mr. Thomas ordered.

"He did it!" Sissy sobbed. She allowed Mr. Thomas to help her up. She twisted her head and neck and then, when she couldn't see, felt over her rump for the long gash in her skirt that exposed her drawers. "That Indian boy! He ran into me!"

It was such an absolute lie, and so deliberately spoken, that Molly had to speak up. "He didn't," she said.

Nobody was listening to her.

"Come upstairs for needle and thread," Miss Lambert instructed Sissy.

"Boy, you've cost more than your day's wage here," Mr. Thomas said. "Your employment is terminated."

Gaston snatched off his tall white hat and threw it into the melee. "If Josiah goes, then I go!"

"Such an action is unnecessary, Gaston," Mr. Thomas insisted.

"Josiah is different, I am different. Josiah is a good worker. I am a good worker. *Et vous êtes …*" Gaston lapsed into his own language.

Molly felt Nell tugging on her skirt. "Come back to work!" Nell hissed.

But Molly had to be heard. Papa would expect it of her. She stepped forward, her sturdy Harvey Girl shoes sliding on bacon grease. She spoke loudly, "It was Sissy. She backed in through the door, and I know you're not supposed to do that. She hit him."

"Ah ha!" Gaston glared at Mr. Thomas.

"That's not true!" Sissy glared at Molly.

"It was indeed the boy who fell first," Miss Lambert pointed out. And they all looked down at Josiah, who still sat where he had fallen, silently awaiting his fate.

"I am in charge of all who work in my kitchen, and Josiah will stay," Gaston stated, as sharp as a knife carving words in the air.

Mr. Thomas sighed. "The boy will stay," he conceded. "Miss Lambert, you will better instruct your girls in the future."

Miss Lambert bowed her head in agreement.

Nell tugged Molly back to the counter. "You shouldn't have done that," Nell whispered. "Sissy won't forget."

Molly didn't care. Sissy wouldn't be part of her life much longer. *Goodbye!* she told the swivel chairs, the day entry, and the night door. *Goodbye!* she told the counter.

As soon as her shift was over, Molly ran upstairs, where Colleen's good black dress hung rejected in the wardrobe. The other Harvey Girls had dressed Colleen up in loaned finery. Nell's best blue jacket, Violet's prettiest striped skirt, Iona's finest hat. Colleen had been a picture when she walked out!

Molly had nothing to do but wait and anticipate. She knew exactly what to expect upon Colleen's return: Colleen's face flushed with pleasure; Colleen's words laced with delight. Colleen would be a portrait of budding love.

But Colleen wasn't. When she finally opened their door, her expression was grim. She looked just the same as that time when Molly and Amy had put damp glue on Jonathan's church pew, ruining his best trousers. "Sissy told me," Colleen said, and instead of going on and on in breathless terms about the delights of her day, she recited the story of the busy-spot accident. But from the wrong point of view!

Molly was forced into the defensive. "It was Sissy who made the boy fall! And then she lied!"

Colleen hardly listened. What she said next was so unexpected, so appalling, that Molly's mouth gaped in horror. "That's not our concern. The rule is, 'We Harvey Girls stick together.'"

"Whose rule?" Molly challenged.

"Everybody's rule. Annis told me." Colleen spoke as

though Annis possessed the tablets of commandment.

"Sissy would have had that boy fired!" Molly insisted.

"That doesn't matter." In the unforgiving New Mexico light, Colleen's eyes appeared more brown than green. No true daughter of Mr. Jerome Gerry of Gerry's Mercantile of Streator, Illinois, would ever be so far removed from truth and charity.

Molly rose from her bed.

"What Annis said, was …" Colleen lectured.

Molly stepped into the hallway and shut the door on her sister's words. She needed someplace to go, a place where she could think. But she could only go downstairs where the kitchen was serving dessert, where the dining room girls were selecting plates of cake, pudding, and little sugar-dusted cookies from the long shelf, where the kitchen boy was scrubbing a huge, encrusted casserole.

She poked her head into the lounge. Miss Lambert was there, drinking tea. "Sit down, Molly," Miss Lambert directed, and Molly had to sit.

Miss Lambert always spoke precisely, with carefully chosen words. Her pronunciation was perfect. She was much like Mr. Latterly, although not quite as dull. "Easterners don't understand the divisions between people that have existed in this territory for the last forty-odd years," she began. "I, myself, dislike the prejudices, but I see few ways of countering them. Do you follow me, Molly?"

Molly had no idea of what Miss Lambert was talking about. "Yes," she replied.

"To oppose these prejudices is to evoke resistance. An obdurate resistance …"

Miss Lambert continued speaking in this way. She might as well have been speaking French. Molly put a schoolroom attentiveness on her face. She waited, waited, waited, and then took her leave as soon as she politely could. She slipped through the green curtain to the counter. Maybe here she could just melt into the background and be alone with herself for a while. But Gravity winked at her as if he'd often been in trouble too. And Violet whispered when passing by, "I don't like Sissy, either. None of us do. But that boy is a half-breed, Molly! You can't go against your own kind."

Molly didn't need the water closet, but that's where she went. She opened the narrow door set beneath the stairs and stayed there as long as she could, until one of the cooks knocked insistently. She had always thought she knew Colleen perfectly. She had never imagined that Colleen could change, far less change for the worse.

Poor Papa!

She had no place to go, no place to think, so she dragged herself back upstairs where Colleen was lounging on her bed, reading a book. Colleen looked so sweet and pretty in her pink wrapper, Molly's hopes resurged. "Wasn't Mr. Latterly just wonderful! Isn't he the *perfect* gentleman?"

"He's very civil." And with those three words, Colleen dismissed the entire day. She said nothing more about Mr. Latterly, their drive, or where they had stopped to eat their boxed lunch. "But you, Molly! I'm gone for less than six hours, and look at what I come back to!" Colleen took one of her calming, deep breaths. "Molly," she said, in a reasoning tone of voice, "I know that Papa taught us to always witness the truth. But here in New Mexico we have to be guided by the other girls. They've been in the West longer. They know what to do, how to act. Jeanette has tried to talk to the kitchen boy and girl about the Bible, and she says they don't want any more to do with us than we want to do with them."

"That doesn't matter," Molly said stubbornly. "It doesn't make wrong right."

Colleen's face shut down. "Put on your nightgown and go to bed," she ordered.

It was the sort of punishment a big sister would give to a thirteen-year-old child, not to a wage-earning, eighteen-year-old woman. But Molly didn't care. Bed was probably the friendliest place for her right now anyway. She got under the covers and listened to Colleen turning pages, to the dining room girls coming upstairs. She lay for hours. And while she lay there, with her eyes closed and her mind furiously awake, she blamed each and every one of the Harvey Girls, most especially Sissy, and next especially Annis. She blamed Miss Lambert, and Josiah, who had never even said *thank you*. She blamed Mr. Thomas and Gaston. She blamed all the citizens of Raton, including Gravity and the other counter regulars. She blamed the passengers whom she served only once and never saw again. The only person she didn't blame was Mr. Latterly.

He was her hope.

Time marched on. Colleen got under her own covers and fell asleep. Molly dozed, imagining her return to Streator. A new house awaited her there, a shipped-from-Chicago house with a leaded-glass front door. The door clicked open. There, and also here. Somebody was coming into Molly's Harvey House room! He? She? was stealthy. The creature walked so as not to disturb the air.

Molly was fully awake now. More than awake. Her every sense was pricklingly alert.

The apparition approached her bed. It didn't touch her. Instead, with silent fingers, it parted the curtains over the window at Molly's feet. It made a small knocking sound as it passed from room to balcony. And then it was less careful. It put on hard-heeled shoes.

Molly's dread transitioned into curiosity. She sniffed. The intruder had been wearing Love Amongst Lilacs cologne. Nell.

With an almost-matching stealth, Molly slid out from under her covers and went to the window herself. It took her several minutes to climb over the windowsill – she was that careful to not awaken Colleen. And then she was outside. On the balcony. In her nightgown. Looking for Nell and not finding her anywhere.

She followed the faded pattern of Nell's noises. After putting on her shoes, Nell had turned left. There had been a scrabbling at the balcony railing. Then a person-climbing-a-ladder sound. How was that possible?

Molly stood at the balcony's south edge. The street below was dim beneath its gas lights, but it wasn't quiet. There were people moving, talking, laughing. Nell. Molly knew Nell's laugh as well as she knew Nell's scent.

Molly put her hands and stomach to the railing and hung over. She didn't see a ladder, but she saw Gaston's trellis, empty of its climbing rose, probably for forever.

"Really!" Molly said to the air.

She went back inside, but not to bed. Instead, she put her pillow against the wall, just beneath the window, and sat there to wait. She dozed. Twice she caught herself from falling over. And then a stockinged foot landed on her shoulder.

Molly grabbed the foot and squeezed it, hard.

"Oh!" Nell gasped.

"Where been?" Molly hissed in counter code.

"Molly, are you all right?" Colleen asked groggily.

"It's just me," Nell said. She grabbed Molly's hand and pulled her into the hallway, then into Iona and Violet's empty room. "Great snakes! Why did you do that?"

"You broke a *rule*!" Molly accused. It felt wonderful to throw that phrase into someone else's face. "You broke curfew!"

"So?" Nell wasn't troubled. "You know Miss Lambert locks the balcony door after we go to bed." Her eyes widened. "You never woke up before? Colleen never told you?"

"Told me what?" Molly demanded.

"About the Midnight Express. That's what we call it. We

all go through that window. Except for Jeanette, who's so holy, and Sissy, who … Well, since *she's* never asked out walking, she keeps *her* window shut so the rest of us can't use it. Colleen says she hasn't yet met anyone who makes her want to risk the trellis, but she doesn't mind our using her window."

"My window," Molly pointed out. Colleen had offered Molly's window without so much as a by-your-leave. "It's my window," Molly fumed.

Nell had no interest in this issue of ownership. She was still surrounded by an aura of love. "I was with Chad Bellamy tonight," she sighed.

And Molly remembered. "He doesn't have fingers."

"That happens to switchmen," Nell defended her beloved. "They often lose fingers when they're attaching cars. But Chad's a brakeman now, and when he becomes a conductor we're going to be married."

"And then you'll go home!" Molly couldn't help but rejoice for Nell.

"Why should I?" said Nell. "No thank you! I came out here to *leave* that hardscrabble farm – and to find a husband. All of us did, except for maybe Jeanette, who only wants to preach at people. Iona came because the only men she knew were sailors, and they so often drown. There weren't any men tall enough in Annis's town. Violet's family wanted her to stay home and take care of her six older brothers. Now, you, you're lucky. You're the only girl I ever heard of who came out West already engaged."

"What?" Were Molly's ears so dirty she wasn't hearing properly? Or could it be possible that this entire episode was actually a dream?

"Colleen told us. She said we should tell all the men. What's your fiancé's name? John?"

"Do you mean *Jonathan*?" Molly must be dreaming. Not even the new Colleen could be *this* perfidious.

"That's it." Nell was pleased with her almost-accuracy. "Leaving him must have been just pitiful," she commiserated. "Colleen says that's why you wouldn't help us out with Faye, that you were simply too sad."

Molly pinched her wrist. She was awake. Very much awake. "I have to go," she said abruptly. And she stormed back to Colleen, whom she shook, fiercely.

"What?" Colleen shot up. "Is it fire?"

"You told people I'm engaged!" Molly raged.

"Oh, that." Colleen settled back down. "I didn't exactly say you were engaged; I said you had a beau. It helped to explain your behavior. And besides, I figured it would stop the customers from looking at you in, well, that way."

"What way?" Molly said through her teeth.

"The 'she's eighteen years old and available' way."

"Me? Available?" Molly almost swallowed her teeth. She got her teeth back and spoke hard enough to bite. "So you let them think I'm engaged?"

"Yes." Colleen wasn't at all remorseful.

"To *Jonathan*?"

"I thought you liked Jonathan."

"That doesn't mean I want to marry him." Molly sharpened her next words into something that might penetrate Colleen's hardened conscience. "You lied!"

Colleen sat back up. "There are lies and there are lies, Molly. I can't expect for you to understand, but I do expect you to follow my lead. Right now you are acting thirteen, which I suppose is all right here in this room, with the door closed. But let me remind you that our food and clothing and shelter are all here within this Harvey House, and within this Harvey House you are to behave as though you are *eighteen*. Now go back to bed!"

Molly went back to bed. This time, the person she blamed the most was Colleen.

→·ᘓᗒ·←

The next morning in the kitchen, Susana actually spoke to Molly while Molly was pouring herself a glass of orange juice. "Thank you for helping my brother."

Finally, Molly thought, *some gratitude.*

Susana gestured toward the sink. Josiah's arms were plunged into dishwater. "My grandmother has made me ask you to a party tonight. I told her you would not come."

Molly tried to sort out the invitation from the dis-invitation.

"Molly." Sissy was on the stairs, too far away to have heard Susana, but close enough to see. Sissy shook her head warningly, as if *she* were the older sister, as if *she* could tell Molly what to do.

All of Molly's wrath from the night before coalesced into one firm gesture. Instead of stepping away from Susana, she stepped closer. "I would love to come," she said. "What time?"

Chapter 6

"Grizzle Guts raised his Winchester and sent Blue Dog to the bone orchard for his heinous act of betrayal." *Billy the Kid and Company*

That evening, when Colleen came upstairs, Molly was already in bed, dressed in her nightgown with the covers pulled up to her chin.

"Are you ill, Molly?" Colleen asked, because it was only a little after seven o'clock.

"No," Molly replied.

Colleen looked down at her, worried and regretful. "I'm sorry we fought. I want you to know that I'm really very proud of you. Nell says you already know everything there is to know about the counter. And Miss Lambert told me that you are 'apt.' That was her word, 'apt.'"

Molly shut her eyes – aptly – and turned her face away – again, aptly. She heard Colleen sigh out a quantity of exasperation.

She heard Colleen undress, then turn the pages of a book for a while, then finally blow out the light. It took forever for Colleen to begin making the little snuffling noises that meant she was falling asleep. And then another forever for her breathing to become slow and even.

Finally, Molly could exit through the window.

She had hidden Mama's dress and her high-buttoned shoes in a corner of the balcony, behind a rocking chair. She only had to pull off her nightgown, because beneath she still wore all of her underclothes, less the hated corset. She was fatter without the corset, so she had to squeeze out all her air before she could hook Mama's skirt.

She sat on the chair to fasten her shoes. Then, flicking aside her nighttime braid, she leaned over the railing to estimate how far down the trellis was. She swung her right leg up, over and down. She reached with her foot, but touched nothing. She was one of the taller Harvey Girls, but even her legs weren't long enough. She would have to hoist herself up onto the railing, sit, and roll over. She did so. She teetered for a moment on her stomach, suddenly beset by qualms. *Should I?* But then she thought of the Harvey Girls, who stuck together. She thought of Colleen, who slept so righteously.

She gave herself up to faith and slid. Her toes touched the trellis. It wobbled, but seemed sturdy enough.

"She comes." A voice from below, a murmur of amazement. Susana.

"She comes," Josiah whispered back.

They were pale faces looking upward.

The sole of Molly's shoe encountered the top of Gaston's rose bush. Now Susana and Josiah were whole bodies, grayed by the gaslights into photographed images of themselves. Other black and gray bodies moved about the moonless street. One waited for Molly to land. He asked, "Where's Nell?"

"Coming," Molly answered. "I suppose." In the shadows of night, Chad Bellamy's hands matched. No missing fingers.

"Do you really wish to come?" Susana inquired.

"Yes." Molly took one last look up at the balcony. She couldn't see her window, which was just as well. Resolutely, she walked between Susana and Josiah. Beyond the gaslights of First Street, the night was an enveloping black. She stepped into nothingness and gasped.

Josiah, then Susana, grasped her elbows. "We will step over a rail," Susana said. Susana's voice sounded friendlier when her face wasn't visible.

Molly stepped over that rail, then others. Her feet crunched through grasses. She could see stars now, millions and millions of stars. There weren't this many stars back in Illinois. The hands at her elbows kept her moving. Sticky grasses pulled at her skirt. She was far enough away from

Raton now that she could smell only grasses. No coal smoke, no engine grease.

A yellow light shone ahead.

"Chihuahua," said Susana. "Our town."

"Our town" was one short street of earthen huts. Oil lamps sent a golden brightness from every wide-open door, from every unshuttered window. A voice shouted words that Molly couldn't understand, and faces filled the windows. People pushed through doorways. Adults, children, even toddlers gathered around Molly as if she were something rare. The women wore bright, satiny skirts. The men boasted up-turned moustaches. The smallest children, garbed in nothing but long shirts, stared at Molly.

And then a very old woman approached, and the citizens of Chihuahua parted as if for Moses, allowing her to pass. She looked Molly over, from Molly's tousled braid to Molly's too-tight shoes. She grinned toothlessly and said …

… More words that Molly couldn't understand. But she understood the gestures. She felt the warmth of the old lady's welcome.

"My grandmother wishes you to know that you are now a friend of Chihuahua," Susana translated. "By your goodness to Josiah, you have been good to us all. Whatever good we can do for you in return, we will."

The old woman was listening, intently. She tapped Susana's arm, sharply.

"Gladly," Susana was forced to add. "We will do good for

you, *gladly.*"

"Gladly." The old woman repeated, her word thick with the sounds of Spanish. Somebody cheered. Others laughed. The littlest children reached out to touch Molly's skirt

"*¡Música!*" somebody called. And someone else strummed a guitar. A man began to sing. His song was both merry and sad, a harmony of contentment and longing, hope and despair.

"*Chocolate.*" This was a word that Molly knew well, but she had never before heard it pronounced with the accent on the *a*. She accepted the cup that a young woman handed her. She sipped. The chocolate too, was a melding of opposites, more bitter than sweet.

Other women began bringing food from their kitchens. Molly tasted it all. She smiled compliments at the beef stewed in tomatoes, at the chicken crusted in sesame seeds, at the cornmeal dumplings, at the fish cooked in something that had to be lime. But when she took a spoonful of a cheese and pepper casserole, her lips opened with a loud and discourteous "Baaagh!" Morsels flew from her mouth. She gasped, trying to cool her tongue. The flame slid down her throat and threatened to scorch her stomach.

Susana pushed a corn pancake into Molly's hand. "Eat," she said. "This will take the sting away."

Molly gobbled. The pain – but it wasn't really pain, it was more like the awakening of a sense she hadn't known she possessed – was somehow absorbed by the pancake. She rolled her tongue around her mouth. There was no damage, but the aftertaste was … "It's good!" she burst out, surprised.

The creator of the casserole, previously dismayed by Molly's reaction, now beamed.

Susana wrinkled her nose at Molly. "You are strange," she stated. It was almost a compliment.

The Chihuahua men were lining up. Molly's stomach was much too full for dancing, but she couldn't refuse. The young men bowed before her, the old men took her hand in a most gallant manner. They swung her from partner to partner. She whirled and swirled. One of her waistband hooks popped, then another. She didn't care. She hadn't had such a wonderful time since, well, since maybe forever!

And then a tornado arrived in the person of Gaston. He blew through the crowd like a wind, strong enough to uproot and toss aside trees. He bowed and kissed Susana's grandmother's hand. He grabbed Molly to lead her in an impossibly fast stamp-hop-twirl. "You are not like the other Harvey Girls!" he boomed. "*Non*! You are not proud for ridiculous reasons. Admit, Susana, I was right. I am always right."

Susana's mouth quirked into a smile.

Molly stumbled – whether from fatigue or the surprise of seeing Susana smile, she didn't know. "Take her back," Gaston commanded. "See that she has no trouble."

This time, Susana took Molly's hand. This time, Josiah pulled the sticky grasses away from Molly's skirt. "Climb carefully," Susana whispered, when they got to Raton. "Go quietly."

Molly climbed up the trellis, over the railing, and landed with a not-too-loud thud on the balcony. She shed her dress and changed back into her nightgown. Cautiously, she stuck her face through the window curtains. Colleen was fast asleep.

→ ⚛ ←

The next morning was different because of the yawns. Molly came downstairs yawning. She found Susana yawning over the orange juice, and Josiah yawning as he set out dining room china on the long serving shelf. Molly poured herself a glass of juice, looked up, and caught Susana's next yawn. Josiah glanced at Molly and caught hers. He spurted a laugh. Molly and Susana giggled, together.

"What's so funny, Molly?" Nell asked.

"Nothing," Molly answered. "Just tired." But she wasn't, really, even though she hadn't done much sleeping for two nights in a row. She poured tea for Gravity, cut up pie for Johnston and listened to the regulars banter. Their topic this morning was the prize bull that Gravity had been expecting.

"It got rustled off in Texas," Jenkins, the freight agent, told the others. "Stolen by someone who for once wasn't Genius Jim."

Molly went through the green curtain to fetch sugar. Gaston arrived to start the dinner preparations with his typical exuberance. "To work! To work! Why are you all so sleepy? To work!" he shouted at his staff. He spun around, caught Molly in his whirlwind and gave her the biggest wink ever. "Wake up!" he bellowed.

So it started out as a good day, and it became even better when Miss Lambert announced, "Molly, I believe you know enough about the counter to train your sister for night work."

Molly shot up both in pride and in height. Miss Lambert was giving her not only the permission, but the authority, to tell Colleen what to do. Molly had never before told Colleen what to do. With relish, she issued orders. "It will be your job to keep the coffee urn filled. And to spoon the brown stuff out of the sugar bowls." She assigned Colleen all the new-girl tasks that Nell and Annis had assigned to her. She made Colleen wipe the counter over and over and over again.

"Good," Miss Lambert commented, on one of her inspection tours.

It was good. It was more than good, it was *amazing*, because Colleen did whatever Molly ordered. Colleen never balked. She didn't once complain. She obeyed Molly as if she, herself, had suddenly become the little sister. "I hadn't realized there was so much to do here," she said. "What next?"

"Refill the donut trays. Bring out more pies," Molly sang.

McCarty had somehow heard of Colleen's new availability – counter girls were more visible than dining room girls. He played truant from his fireman job to come linger with the regulars. He leaned so far over the counter he was almost in Harvey Girl territory. His sleeves dripped bits of coal into other people's cups.

"Miss Colleen!" he said. "Will yaw be here all the time now?"

And Molly hastily imparted another lesson. "Three words!"

But Colleen kept her distance, just as she should. "It's temporary," she told McCarty. She pulled out a clean cup, poured McCarty's coffee, and moved on to another customer.

Molly was so pleased with her sister, she said, "You're doing just fine."

"Gotta clean up, some," Johnston advised McCarty.

"Ladies don't like to be given more work to do." Gravity indicated the dark dust on McCarty's section of the counter.

"Genius Jim once used a disguise," said Jenkins, and they were off again, on another tale.

Molly stood back, as Nell sometimes did, to view the counter from a distance – as one picture, as one working unit. The counter possessed a dance of its own, she now realized, just like the kitchen. The counter dance was a sort of reel, with intricate do-si-dos and a special "ladies' left." The regulars' banter provided both percussion and song. And it was she, Molly Gerry, who was now calling the steps.

> ⚜ ⚜

Molly might have suspected that Chihuahua was a dream – the colors were so bright in her memory, the tastes so sharp, the music so pure. Except that now, the kitchen welcomed her. Whenever she stepped in – and after Colleen's first day at the counter, Molly resumed coffee-fetching duty just so that she *could* step in – she was enveloped into Gaston's hurricane as if she had always been part of his energy. There he was, the eye of the culinary storm. There was Susana, a constant, trailing breeze, picking up whatever he dropped or shed. There was Josiah, elbow-deep in dishwater, a sort of soapy rain-maker. And there was Molly, wending her way through, grinning at Gaston while he roared, seeing Susana roll her eyes behind Gaston's back in complicit amusement, nodding at Josiah's friendly shrug of recognition. The other cooks, whether baker or fry, didn't count. They were just nameless bursts of industry on the outskirts of the place that really mattered: that spot of creative perfection directly beneath Gaston's flying hands.

Molly couldn't always see what was happening beneath Gaston's fingers, but she could smell. And she could observe what was served to the dining room customers, and only rarely to the counter. The rare exception was Gravity, who sometimes preferred to eat fine food on heavy china, and who lingered on his stool over a dinner of quail roasted in grape leaves while his fellow regulars were content with meatloaf sandwiches.

"The quail are from Gravity's own ranch," Colleen whispered in Molly's ear. "But the grapes come from California." Colleen somehow always knew that sort of thing. She knew facts of which Molly, up until now, had been unaware. Such as, "Gaston's not from France, but from Louisiana." And, "He's a Creole cook." Whatever that meant.

"Gaston studied at the magazine *Cordon Bleu*!" Here Colleen swallowed the ends of the last two words as if she too could speak French.

Molly didn't have time to ask what kind of school a magazine was. She had to get Soffit's eggs on rye with two pieces of ham, plus an extra pickle.

"Mr. Harvey," when Colleen said that name, she became as glassy-eyed with admiration as the old man in the Kansas City depot had been, "pays his cooks as much, even more, than what big-city bankers earn. Can you imagine?"

Molly couldn't. Gaston didn't seem that fine. He wasn't nearly as fine as Gravity, for whom he made special meals. He wasn't even as fine as Sheriff Armbruster, who wore a huge buckle made of solid silver with a nugget of turquoise in the center as big as a turkey egg. Gaston was just Gaston, blustery and blowy and loud, loud, loud. The kind of person who could make a meringue you only had to touch with the tip of a fork before it crumbled.

Gaston represented the pinnacle of Harvey House excellence.

Molly was now "very good," which is what Miss Lambert judged after Colleen had been a week at the counter. "Very good, Molly. I believe you are both ready for the night shift. You will commence tomorrow."

Colleen was thrilled by Molly's new evaluation. What thrilled Molly was finding an envelope on her pillow after they went upstairs. Mail! Her first! *I miss you*, Amy wrote. *We all do. Jonathan and I talk about you all the time. I'm taking piano lessons. Did you know that Jonathan sings? He has a very nice voice.* In a spasm of homesickness, Molly clutched the single page to her heart.

Colleen also had a missive that she was reading with far less passion.

"Who's it from?" Molly inquired.

"Mr. Latterly."

In a moment, Molly's longing had transfigured into a hope that expanded, exploded, then tingled the air of their bedroom with its own kind of lightning. "What does he say?"

Colleen handed the letter over. "You may read it if you wish."

My dear Miss Gerry – Mr. Latterly had written on the train between Barstow and San Bernardino, California. *Thank you for your company during my recent visit to Raton. You will be interested to know that Barstow is exactly one thousand six hundred and forty-five miles from the Missouri River ...* How could he know so much? And why did he have to share it? *I beg that you will honor me by continuing this correspondence.* Finally! He had come to the point!

"You must write back to him immediately," Molly rejoiced.

"Yes," Colleen mused. "I will." She was buttoning her nightgown. "Soon," she muttered. She reached for her hairbrush, her forehead puckering with thought.

Molly sat cross-legged on her bed, watching. Colleen was

so pretty nowadays. Her New Mexico expression was soft, her eyes were bright, her manner was lively. Working as a Harvey Girl was obviously much easier than taking care of Papa. "Very good." Molly truly deserved the commendation. She deserved more, she deserved an accolade. She deserved "Wonderful!" because taking care of a salesman husband would be easiest of all.

At first, Molly thought working nights would be like having seven days off in a row, with empty mornings and freed-up afternoons. That first day she came down for breakfast at ten o'clock instead of just before six. She didn't want a sandwich, so she gathered up bread, coffee, and a slice of ham. She was heading toward the lounge when Gaston motioned to a little stool set against the stove-side wall. This was the stool that Susana sometimes stood on to reach the highest shelves. "Sit," he commanded.

Molly sat, a witness and a point within the compass of Gaston's noise and energy. "*Choco-la-te*," she murmured, trying to pronounce the word in the Spanish way. Gaston was making a chocolate sauce.

He swirled by with a pot and a spoon. He stopped. "Taste," He put the dripping spoon against Molly's lips.

Susana had a napkin on Molly's lap before a single drop hit her skirt.

"What is it?" Gaston queried.

"Chocolate," Molly said in the English way.

"More!" Gaston insisted.

Molly let the flavor sit on her tongue, soak into her memory – mix and match in her mind like colors from a paint box. "Orange," she said. "And … licorice?"

"Ah!" Gaston was pleased. "Give her an apron!"

Susana pulled Molly from the stool. She wrapped a big kitchen apron around Molly's waist. "The licorice is called anise," she said. "Come."

"Come" meant "follow." Molly followed Susana, who followed Gaston, and as a line of three they wove through the kitchen. Susana picked up whatever Gaston dropped. She pointed. It was Molly's job to restore the item to its proper place. Molly learned where the ladles were hung, where the baking sheets were stored, where the anise was kept. Soon she was part of a kitchen team, creating a pudding with caramel nuggets and a chocolate sauce that was faintly citric, faintly memoried with flavors from a candy store.

It was delicious.

Six p.m. came, and Molly had to become a Harvey Girl again. She went to the counter to take over from Annis, who had returned to her old job for this one week. Colleen had already relieved Nell. The routine was nothing new. Coffee, donuts, sandwiches. The last train passengers arrived for the last half-hour meal. Local men, newly off duty, ordered supper. Then the main entry to the Harvey House was locked, and Mr. Thomas unlocked the night door in the counter room.

One, two, three men wandered in. Molly went into the kitchen for coffee. The assistant cooks were gone, and only Gaston, Susana and Josiah remained. "Now," Gaston announced, "we will spell."

"Molly!" Colleen called.

The Buttercup's crew had returned home. They wanted roast beef sandwiches, sliced turkey with gravy, steak and eggs. It was the newly arrived night cook who provided, not Gaston. Gaston continued to drill Susana and Josiah. "Quince!" he challenged them.

"Molly!" Colleen called.

The Buttercup crew was disappointed to hear that there was no more ice cream. They consoled themselves with Oregon pears. "Tell Miss Colleen about Gallup," Soffit urged McCarty.

McCarty needed no urging. He spread coal dust left and right with his gestures. "Ain't no place prettier, Miss Colleen! Rocks red and white and gray! There's some as say the desert ain't got no look to it. But I say, ain't no place prettier."

Molly took over the task of serving McCarty. Only he was disappointed. The Buttercup crew finally finished their meals and left.

In the kitchen the night cook was all alone, spreading out a game of solitaire on the table where Susana had so recently been spelling.

"Molly!" Colleen called.

Talmadge, the night telegrapher, wanted a pot of coffee

to carry back to the depot post office. Only three men sat at the counter, and they were dozing. The trickle of customers through the night door diminished, then stopped. Molly put her hand over Papa's hidden watch. Her palm felt the ticking, no slower than usual. Still, time dragged. Midnight passed, then one a.m. Molly found herself falling asleep while serving coffee. She apologized to her customer, a man from the roundhouse, that great, curved, locomotive stable. He was an engine wiper. Molly could tell that by the grease he was leaving on the dishes. Grease that Josiah would have to scrub away tomorrow.

What was he doing up so late? Why were these other men staying up so late?

Molly sponged the spilled coffee. She took orders from the crew of a night train bringing lumber over Raton Pass. She tried hard to stay awake. But at four in the morning, when the baker arrived to start his work, she was lulled into dreams by the odors of yeast, sugar and fruit. She stood, leaning against the cup shelf, and saw pies, endless pies, Alice-in-Wonderland pies, dancing do-si-dos behind her shut eyelids.

She slept long into the following afternoon. When she got downstairs, by the time she sat on the stool with her breakfast-lunch in her lap, Gaston was well into his second menu of the day. He snatched away her plate – those bits of pimento chicken she had been able to scrape from the warming pan. "No, no!" he insisted. "You will taste!"

She wrapped herself in an apron. She took her place

behind Susana. She ate while Gaston cooked.

This evening's special was macaroni, but of a kind that Molly had never seen before. Big and hollow noodles that the assistant cooks boiled and that Susana cut open. Molly was allowed to stir the stuffing, to taste when Gaston did. "What?" he asked her, again and again. "Not chicken liver," he corrected. "Goose!" "Not mushroom, truffle!"

She had tasted truffles before, in a chicken dish during her first week of work. The goose liver was richer, meatier, than chicken. She put each flavor into her memory, where it placed itself like a gradation of color.

"Do you enjoy?" Gaston asked over his shoulder, as he roared from stuffing to sauce. Molly understood. Did she enjoy the tasting? Did she enjoy the cooking?

"I do!"

"Boil out the sherry," he taught, "but not the Madeira."

Sherry. Madeira. The rainbow of tastes in her memory grew broader and brighter.

That evening, she used every excuse to be in the kitchen. She reclaimed the tasks of refilling the cream pitchers, the sugar bowls, the cup shelf, the silverware tray, and the salt and pepper shakers. After Gaston left, and with the night cook ignoring her, she toured Gaston's domain. She touched his tools of trade: the knife that was sharp enough to slice truffles paper thin; the grinder that turned meat into paste; a little pot reserved for melting butter and nothing else.

When midnight came, she was still thinking about food.

"Did Mama cook?" she asked Colleen.

"Mama was an excellent cook," Colleen replied.

"What did she make?"

Colleen listed. "Cakes and pies and roasts and …"

The ghost of a crispy sweetness melted over Molly's tongue. "Honey chicken?"

"Yes." Colleen laughed. "You used to love Mama's honey chicken."

The next evening, during spelling time, when Gaston invited Molly to sit at the kitchen table, just for a minute, next to Susana, she told him about the honey chicken. "Afterward, Papa hired cooks," Molly finished. "Most of them weren't very good."

"That was because they did not care," said Susana, who was always careful with her spelling.

"They did not want success," said Josiah, who worked so hard at dishwashing that his arms were permanently red and chapped.

"They felt not the art," Gaston opined from his position of established expert. He smiled upon Molly with fatherly pride. "They had not the *goût*." He gathered all the fingers of one hand and touched them to his lips so that that Molly would understand. *Taste*.

>⊰϶⊱<

Colleen was almost as energetic as Gaston the following day. She proposed a project – new clothes for Molly.

"Something we can do together!" she said. Molly couldn't resist Colleen's good humor. They went shopping at Dacy's mercantile.

There wasn't much to choose from. Molly's new skirt would have to be blue serge, her shirtwaist white percale. But Colleen insisted on talking over every detail – length and pockets and plackets and tucks. She had Molly help her prepare the lounge for sewing. Molly rolled the heavy sewing machine from a dark corner to the window. Colleen closed the door to the kitchen and began measuring Molly all over.

"I'll double the cuffs to allow room for your arms to grow," Colleen planned. "I'll knit a sweater for you during our late nights at the counter. We'll buy a winter coat from Mr. Dacy. Today I'll show you how to cut out the skirt. Molly?" Molly's hand was on the lounge doorknob. "We're going to cut!"

"You don't really need me," Molly begged off. Today Gaston was making a Pineapple Bavarian Cream.

"Indeed I do." Colleen's voice had changed. No longer sisterly and sharing, it had reverted to being big-sisterly and bossy. What Colleen had been before coming to the counter. "I don't want you spending so much time in the kitchen."

Molly's spine went rigid. "Why?"

"Something about what you are doing there seems so, well, young," Colleen accused.

"I *am* young!" Molly answered back.

"People might suspect," Colleen retorted.

"As long as I work as hard as I do, why should they? I'm *very good*. Remember?"

Colleen backed off, a little. "What am I supposed to say if people ask?" she argued.

"Tell them," Molly replied with Gaston-like grandiosity, "that I am learning how to cook." She swept out of the lounge, unfortunately almost colliding with Sissy in the busy spot.

"Watch yourself!" Sissy snarled.

Molly wrapped herself in a kitchen apron. She fumbled the knot and had to tie it twice.

"You are darkness itself today," Gaston observed. "A cloud about to rain in my kitchen. When Susana is angry I make her chop. But you, I think, should stir. We will need a whipped cream."

Molly remembered where the cream whip was kept. She chose a bowl. She took cream from the ice box and poured until Gaston said, "Stop." She added powdered sugar. Then she beat and beat and beat.

"Sometimes we can change things. Sometimes we cannot," Gaston said philosophically.

Molly's arm was sore. "I have a plan," she told him. "I have a plan that will solve *everything*."

But shortly after midnight, Colleen revealed that she had decided not to write to Mr. Latterly. "Although I'm grateful for his esteem."

Molly had never imagined such a possibility. "What?" She was stunned.

"I don't want to encourage him," Colleen explained. "I don't want him to think something exists that doesn't."

Amidst the ashes of her hope, Molly grasped for sparks. "Is it McCarty?" She would work on McCarty. She might be able to mold him to her plan.

"McCarty? No! I know he pays attention, but I could never encourage McCarty. No, I'm just not interested right now. There's enough to do, settling into our new life. Getting better acquainted with our friends. I don't think I'll want a beau for a very long time."

"I see," said Molly. "Excuse me." She left the counter as if running to the water closet. Instead, she detoured into the kitchen where the night cook was lying on the table, napping. She reached beneath his snores to pull open the table drawer. She removed a piece of the white paper that Gaston used for baking tarts and cakes. She found Susana's pencil. She returned to the counter, served donuts to a crew from over the Pass and cleared a spot where she could work.

Colleen picked up her knitting. "Jeanette asked me why you prefer Mexicans and half-breeds," she began conversationally, as if she had just happened to pick up a new topic along with her needles.

Molly closed her ears. She leaned against the counter and composed.

Dear Mr. Latterly,

How grateful I was to receive your communication. And how pleased I will be to continue our correspondence. I must ask, however, that you address your envelopes to my sister, Molly. As she is already engaged, other people will not wonder at the volume of mail she receives. It will be our secret, shared amongst the three of us.

Your sincere friend,
Colleen Gerry

Chapter 7

"Stories of Western conflict are greatly exaggerated."
The Atchison, Topeka and Santa Fe Railway Guidebook

So it was war, and a dreadful one, thought Molly. She and
Colleen had never fought before, not for so long, never
about something so important. And even in those smaller
skirmishes, Molly had never won. Yet she persisted.

When their night shift ended, and they returned to their
day jobs, it was as though Molly could breathe again. Nell
didn't mind if Molly lingered in the kitchen, not as long as
Molly appeared at the counter when needed. Molly developed
something of a sixth sense, a way of hearing when the counter
volume rose to a critical point. When Nell needed another

pair of hands, Molly was there.

But at bedtime, Colleen harped, and harped, and harped. "That boy is an Indian," she said.

This was when Molly was putting on her nightgown. Slowly, resolutely, she pushed her face up through the neckline. "Half," she said, in her calmest voice. "Josiah is half Indian, just like Susana's half Mexican. Their father was an American. He left. Susana's mother died. Josiah's mother ran off with another American. Susana's grandmother ended up taking care of them both."

Colleen wasn't sidetracked. "I want you to find more suitable friends," she persisted.

Poof! went all of Molly's pretense at calmness. "Where?" she fumed. "Who? Johnston? Gravity? Jenkins?" She opened, then slammed, the door to their room. She had hoped to find air in the hallway, but Sissy was there in her nightgown. And Nell, all dressed up for taking the Midnight Express.

"Well, if it isn't Miss Vanderbilt from Ill-annoy," Sissy remarked.

"Leave her alone, Sissy," Nell said testily.

"Or should I say," Sissy simply wouldn't stop, "our newest kitchen maid?"

"She's learning how to cook," Nell defended Molly. "That's something engaged women have to know how to do. You'd understand if you'd ever had a beau."

Sissy's nose became pinched at the corners. She opened her mouth to spit out more insults. Molly didn't wait to hear.

She ran down to the kitchen.

Her friends were gone, but the air was still thick with the spices from Gaston's chicken Creole. Molly inhaled as much of the lingering pepper as she could. Heat met heat. It pushed her internal pressure down. She blew out, long and hard. When Gaston was irritated, he blew off steam. In, out, in, out, until Molly's lungs were clear and clean. In, out, in, out, until they ballooned with a fierce determination. She went upstairs to confront Colleen. This time she wielded her voice like a kitchen knife. "If I am eighteen years old in this Harvey House, then I am old enough to make friends with whomever I want. And the people I choose are Gaston, Susana and Josiah."

Colleen wrung her hands, twisting them like tea towels that needed to be shed of water. "Someone will guess!" she fretted.

"They won't," Molly promised. "Ever."

And she was as good as her word. She was scrupulous. She never did anything, inside the kitchen or out, that would lead people to think she wasn't exactly as old as Colleen claimed her to be. During evening hours in the kitchen she rarely talked, lest she reveal too much. Mostly, she listened. Josiah's goal was to become a locomotive engineer. "Very hard to do," Gaston said. "Especially for an Indian boy. You must study! Molly will help."

Molly helped by becoming a spelling coach. While Gaston had an impressive vocabulary in five languages for food, only

Molly knew that locomotive was spelled with three *os*.

"Engine, brakes, tender," she recited, while Josiah washed dishes. "When you spell 'freight,' don't forget the *g* and the *h*."

"English makes no sense," Josiah grumbled.

"Ha! French is worse," Gaston said, as if that was something to be proud of. "But to spell well, you must read."

"I have a book," Molly remembered. She dashed upstairs and brought *Billy the Kid and Company* back down to the kitchen table. She read the first page out loud. Josiah was not impressed. "Who wrote that?" he asked. "He knows nothing of New Mexico!"

Still, Josiah now stayed even later into the evenings, sitting with Molly at the table and reading slowly and haltingly from her book. He grumbled at what he said were exaggerations or obvious untruths. But he worked with a determination Molly had never seen in her Streator friends. Jonathan attended a proper school with a real teacher, but he came nowhere close to matching Josiah's initiative.

"You can't teach a monkey to read," Sissy once commented, passing through.

But when Miss Lambert saw, she approved. "Excellent!" she said. "I applaud you, Molly. Come with me. I have something that will help."

Molly had to follow. She had to ascend the stairway behind Miss Lambert's mauve linen skirt. She had to turn right, instead of left, in the hallway above.

Miss Lambert opened her office door and lit the gas.

Molly saw a desk, a pile of papers, and three bookshelves all filled with books. While Miss Lambert perused titles, Molly spied. The framed diploma on the wall read, *Wellesley College.* The sheet of paper covered with precise penmanship in the exact center of Miss Lambert's desk began, *The Ute Indians occupy the northern section of…*

"I own two." Miss Lambert startled Molly away from *the northern section of…* "You may use this dictionary as long as it proves useful."

"Thank you." Molly accepted the dictionary. She retraced her steps with triumph, encountering Nell, Annis, Jeanette and Sissy, who had popped their heads out of their rooms to watch and speculate. She held the dictionary high so that they all could see.

Josiah loved the dictionary. He turned the pages slowly, hunting. "Drawbar. Caboose." He pressed down with his pencil, copying words onto Gaston's paper. "This," he said, "is real."

That night at bedtime, Colleen questioned Molly as closely and as carefully as Gaston dissected an artichoke. "Miss Lambert gave you a dictionary," she mused. "I can tell the other girls you have a dream of becoming a teacher. That should explain everything!"

So now Molly was a teacher, as well as being an engaged woman learning how to cook.

Gaston had begun to create autumn desserts. Persimmon pudding, walnut torte, pomegranate sherbet. Susana moaned at the prospect of making pomegranate juice, but Molly volunteered. After working hours, when everybody was gone, she stood at Josiah's washing sink and picked thousands of pomegranate pips from their honeycomb-like shells. She crushed the tiny pips against a sieve with a spoon, dripping a thin stream of juice into the waiting bowl. She worked as the hours stretched, while the night cook played endless games of solitaire. He never talked, which suited Molly just fine. This was the one place in all of New Mexico where she didn't have to be somebody or something other than herself.

She came to crave that little circle of silence – the pomegranates, the sieve, the spoon. Every evening she went straight from the counter, to the kitchen, to the sink, not bothering to change out of her uniform. Too often, the pale pink juice soaked through her kitchen apron to the Harvey Girl apron underneath. Too often, she didn't notice the stain.

Miss Lambert did. The first time Miss Lambert caught Molly with a dirty apron at the counter, she was critical. "How could you not see it? Go upstairs and change."

The second time, Miss Lambert was sharp.

The third time, Miss Lambert visited Molly's room. "I did not mind telling you once about your apron. But Molly, it displays absolute obstinacy on your part to have to be told three times."

Molly's breath caught in her throat. Instinctively, she turned to Colleen.

And Colleen didn't fail her. "Molly doesn't only like to

teach, she likes to learn, Miss Lambert," Colleen lied glibly.
"She is making up for the education she had to forgo when
our father died. In her zeal, she sometimes becomes forgetful."

"Well," Miss Lambert relented. "Even a scholar must
abide by the rules. Clean aprons, Molly, always." And she left.

"Thank you!" Molly exhaled.

"You're welcome." Colleen burrowed deep under her
covers. Her next words, when they came, weren't unkind, but
still, they contained a warning. "You've forced me to rely on
you, Molly. Be discrete, always!"

The following morning, when Molly laced up her corset,
she squeezed herself not only into the body, but into the heart,
mind and soul of a much older self. She remained that self all
day, not truly breathing until late at night when, untying the
strings, she was finally able to shed all of Colleen's lies.

→ ❧ ←

It was Gaston who decided that Molly and Susana
should take their midday breaks together. "This one," he said,
speaking of Susana, "doesn't have time to be with other girls in
Chihuahua." He shooed them out onto the porch.

So now, in the late mornings, before the dinner rush
began, Molly usually ate a picnic of counter food with Susana.
They sat on the porch steps wrapped in a shawl (Susana) and
a Colleen-knitted sweater (Molly), talking about Streator
(Molly) and Chihuahua (Susana). They watched the world of
Raton go by.

When Mr. Latterly responded to "Colleen's" letter, Molly *had* to tell somebody. She couldn't help but mention, "My sister's beau has written!"

"I did not know Colleen had a beau," was Susana's comment.

Molly found her mouth suddenly glued shut by a confusing mixture of truth and lies. She worked it open. "Colleen doesn't, either."

Susana wrinkled her brow.

It was easier to tell the truth. The truth about Colleen, if not about anything else. "You mustn't tell a soul," Molly insisted.

"I will not," Susana promised.

"I have a plan."

Susana listened carefully. When Molly was finished, Susana nodded with such conviction that Molly was startled. "Mr. Latterly will come," Susana declared. "He will come, and he will fulfill all of your dreams. This could be a great romance. I will help. What does the gentleman write?"

Molly read aloud, "*My dear Miss Gerry, I have been to Streator and am happy to report a successful harvest this year, with a countywide average yield of forty bushels of corn per acre.*" After describing the harvest, Mr. Latterly estimated the cost of repairing Main Street in front of the stablery, "*where rental horses have badly damaged the bricks.*" He went on to compliment the timeliness of the train that returned him to Chicago. "*With all my best wishes, Hugh Latterly.*"

"Oh, no!" Susana cried. "No-no-no-no-no! That will not do! That will not do at all! Mr. Latterly must *sing* when he thinks of Colleen! He must write *poetry*! Colleen will inspire him."

So the next morning, they sat knee to knee on the porch while sparrows pecked at their crumbs. Molly braced a sheet of kitchen paper against the back of *Billy the Kid and Company*, and wrote while Susana dictated. "*My dear Mr. Latterly, your letter made the sun shine for me today.*" They were so engrossed they didn't hear Violet return from an errand across the street.

"Your words were like flowers in my mind?" Violet repeated Susana's next phrase. "What on earth does that mean?"

Molly and Susana collapsed with laughter. Violet touched Molly's head in passing. "Such a silly girl!" she said kindly.

Mr. Latterly responded to Susana's letter right away. "*I have unfortunately broken my leg in a fall from a ladder,*" Molly read out loud, "*and must convalesce here in Chicago.*"

"Good!" Susana was pleased. "Colleen will tell him that her own leg aches in sympathy with his. She will say that every step she walks is a hope that he will soon run to her door." Susana composed her thoughts. "*My heart clamors to comfort you during these days of pain and distress.*"

It was turning into a lovely correspondence. At least from Colleen's side. After two or three letters, Mr. Latterly finally allowed himself to relax to the point of addressing her as "Colleen" instead of "Miss Gerry." Since "Colleen" had been addressing him as "dear Hugh" from almost the beginning, Molly and Susana thought Mr. Latterly tardy but, in the end, tractable.

"He must be lonely, all shut up with that broken leg," Molly sighed. If only Mr. Latterly had injured himself here in Raton, giving Colleen the chance to nurse him back to health, giving the two of them the chance to fall in love in a more natural way.

"Impossible," Susana said crisply. "He would bore Colleen to death before he could walk with a cane. No, this is better. This way we hear all of his facts and figures. She does not have to. By the time he returns to Raton, he will be calling her "dear Colleen." His love will be so great, your sister will have no choice but to succumb to his ardent proposals."

What a wonderful daydream! Mr. Latterly finally tossing aside his crutches to rush out West. Mr. Latterly entering the Harvey House wearing a new suit and hat, looking distinguished. Well, at least recognizable. Mr. Latterly dropping to his knees before Colleen, telling her …

"*Affection from afar is a pull that cannot be resisted*," Susana dictated.

It was a very sustaining daydream.

Molly made envelopes from pieces of kitchen paper. She addressed them carefully to Hugh Latterly, c/o George Jamison, Optical Lenses. She never left the envelopes on the lounge table for Miss Lambert to take to the depot as the other Harvey Girls did. She always took the envelopes to the postal window herself. She made arrangements to pick up her mail there too.

"Miss Molly!" The postmaster, like everyone else in town, knew her well. "Another letter for your fiancé?"

"Yes." It was starting to become an easy lie. Sometimes it seemed less a lie than a story.

"Colleen must tell Mr. Latterly a tale of love, to help him through the long hours of convalescence," Susana decided. She settled into her imagination. "*Once there was a beautiful young lady whose heart opened like a wound at the thought of her lover's absence.*"

"This is good!" Molly breathed. "Slow down. I have to cross something out."

She copied the letter immediately after her shift, while sitting on the kitchen stool. Her best penmanship – midway in skill between Miss Lambert's and Josiah's – filled three pages. The Harvey Girls swished in and out, taking food and dishes from the long shelf. Molly heard something drop. She looked over to see a fork on the floor and Sissy crouching to retrieve it. Sissy ostentatiously maintained her pose, staring at Molly's calves beneath her ever-shortening uniform skirt. The girls behind Sissy, their rhythm broken, were stopped in an impatient queue.

"My, my, Miss Molly," Sissy drawled. "Still growing like a little child?"

Molly froze. She couldn't lift her pen from the paper.

Annis saved her, "I didn't reach full height until I was

almost twenty," Annis growled. "Move, Sissy!"

"Move, Sissy!" Violet seconded, adding, "you can only see so low because you're so short."

Sissy sniffed, but moved. Annis winked at Molly. Violet gave Molly a conspiratorial smile.

Molly found that she could lift her pen again. The ink had splotched, but that didn't matter. She had barely started the fourth page. She continued on another sheet. *They were wed in a chapel that was blessed by roses, entwined with grape vines, and leafed with their every heart's desire.*

⇥ ❧ ⇤

Colleen had begun to read books. It was Miss Lambert's fault. Nowadays, when Molly went upstairs at bedtime, she almost always found her sister on her bed, in her pink wrapper, reading. If Colleen wasn't in their room, she was down the hall in Miss Lambert's office, talking and laughing. What those two had to laugh about, Molly couldn't imagine.

At night, Colleen had begun to say surprising things. Things like, "I might have gone to college. Maybe. If I had thought of it back then. Papa might not have wanted it. What do you think, Molly?"

Molly had no opinion at all. She was always too tired from work, kitchen, spelling, letter writing, and pomegranates.

The worst evenings were when Colleen wanted to read aloud. "*But neither the business alleged, nor the magnificent compliment, could win Catherine from thinking that some very different object must occasion so serious a delay of proper repose.*" Such a jumble of words! Such tangled phrases! Molly practically needed scissors in order to understand.

One evening, after a particularly grueling day, Molly stopped at the top of the stairs to listen for Colleen's voice. She heard no laughter – none at all, not from anybody, anywhere. How odd! The hallway was completely empty. No girls leaned against the walls in various stages of dress and undress, gossiping and joking. Instead, every door was firmly shut. How unfriendly!

While Molly puzzled this out, two of the girls simultaneously left their rooms: Nell, dressed for walking, and Sissy, with a water pitcher in her hand.

Sissy spoke first. "All dressed up like a sore finger," she flung out, with her usual sourness. "Carrying on with a half-handed man."

Nell gasped. "You cow!"

Sissy was swift in return, "You chippie!"

This was far nastier than the usual Sissy confrontations. But the insults stopped right there. Sissy circled Molly and stalked off downstairs.

"You cow?" Molly repeated. She had never heard Nell use that expression before.

"Oh, Molly." Nell was exasperated. "Twig up! Open your eyes! While you've been cooking, things have been happening."

"Like what?" Molly asked.

"Violet has a beau."

"Oh." That didn't seem so very significant.

"A *serious* beau," Nell emphasized. "A real brick of a man, the *marrying* kind. A rancher. He only eats in the dining room. And he's almost as rich as Gravity! Well, nobody's as rich as Gravity."

"Does he want to go home?" Had Molly missed out on a likely candidate? "Are they going East?"

"Molly!" Nell reached for Molly's shoulder and shook it. "Listen to me! A rich man is crazy for Violet. She's all over the moon about him. And Sissy is pea-green with envy. That means nobody, but nobody, can be easy upstairs."

"Oh." Finally, Molly understood.

Violet's voice sounded from behind her door. "It's not my fault, and I'm not sorry for it!" The words were muffled.

"Of course not." Nell raised her own voice to speak through the pinewood barrier. "Sissy was born short as a pie crust."

"Are you saying that she's mean? Or that she isn't tall?" Iona poked her nose out, which was unfortunate, because Sissy was returning from the kitchen.

"Maybe short, but not fat," Sissy said pointedly. "Was it because *you* were in the boat with him, Iona, that your man drowned?"

Iona flushed so red, Molly feared she might die right then and there. Violet's arms pulled Iona away. "At least Iona had a chance at marriage," Violet yelled. "Unlike *you*."

"I don't see them standing in line wanting her now," Sissy

shouted back.

Iona pushed past Violet to stumble downstairs. Molly heard the water closet door shut, then the unmistakable sound of vomiting.

"Unforgivable," Violet screamed at Sissy. "Unforgivable!"

At that, every door opened. Everybody but Annis and Jeanette, who were down at the counter, joined the fray. "Silence!" Miss Lambert commanded. "Silence!" She repeated that word until she held them all quiet with her gaze. "We will have a meeting, *now*."

Miss Lambert sent Violet to ask Mr. Thomas to come watch the counter. She had Molly and Colleen set extra chairs in the lounge. She forced her girls to sit shoulder-to-shoulder around the table. Uniformed Annis and Jeanette, Molly in a kitchen apron, Nell and Violet in walking clothes, Iona and Sissy in nightgowns, Colleen in her wrap.

"This happens every year," Miss Lambert began. "This disaccord, this strain. I know you each think it is another girl's fault, but it isn't. It's the season. This is the time of year when homesickness can become dangerous. Do not take your unhappiness out on each other. Instead, remember the reasons for these holidays. Thanksgiving. The embodiment of absolute love. Do not let your love for your families, or your longing for your homes, shrink you into bitterness. Allow yourselves to search for friendship and comfort amongst each other. Give to each other what you cannot give to those who are now so far away."

It was a fine speech, better than any sermon. Violet cried.

Jeanette sat erect, for she had adhered to these precepts all along. "*Love thy neighbor as thyself*," she murmured. Iona was meek. Annis was thoughtful. Nell resigned. Colleen nodded agreement with her educated friend's every word. And Sissy, the cause of all the disaccord, said, "Oh, all right."

Oh, all right. It wasn't a heart-felt concession. But most likely, it would be enough.

Chapter 8

"Genius Jim took a bullet to the throat — and survived."
Billy the Kid and Company

The Harvey Girls weren't alone in their homesickness. That became obvious on Thanksgiving Day when Mr. Thomas had small tables for four placed in the entry vestibule and in front of the counter. The railroaders who brought the tables in from storage sniffed the air like dogs.

"Roast turkey!" McCarty sighed. Molly had never seen him scrubbed so clean of coal dust. "My ma could roast a turkey angels would fight over."

"Smells like home," Chad Bellamy yearned. "Where's Nell?"

"Working," Molly replied.

All the girls were working extra hard today. It was a Full House, but not of AT&SF passengers. The customers were the regulars from both the counter and the dining room: railroaders, cowboys, miners. They arrived washed and cologned, their carbolic soap and sandalwood scents competing with the aroma of Gaston's best American-inspired cuisine. The men came dressed in their finest, which for some meant waistcoats and jackets, and for others new hats and oversized, shiny belt buckles. They sat in a groomed and polished row at the counter, in mannerly groups at the extra tables. And they were grateful.

"Thank you, miss," they said again and again, as Molly, Nell and Annis, today's counter girls, served them the most important meal of the year. "Talk to your plates, boys!" a rancher said loudly, and every head bent in mumbled prayer.

On this day, everybody ate the same meal. Six courses, from oysters to pie. There was no ordering. Molly had only to take plates from the shelf, set them down, and clear them away.

"Mr. Newton," – it took a moment before she realized that Johnston was addressing Gravity – "can I swing you some gravy?"

They were models of decorum, these recently-scrubbed, Sunday-garbed men. They passed butter, salt, and biscuits with grave courtesy. They please'd and thank you'd like children in an etiquette class. "You eat with this, Joe." A prospector waved his fork to catch his partner's attention. "You don't swaller fine vittles from a knife." With forks, or with spoons, they ate their slices of mincemeat and pumpkin pie. They drank their coffee. Then they exited through the vestibule door, tipping their hats. "Thank you, sir," they said to Mr. Thomas.

Mr. Thomas locked the door behind them. He turned to the Harvey Girls, who had gathered to watch the last of their customers go. "Miss Lambert?" he said.

"Upstairs, girls," Miss Lambert directed. "Mr. Thomas and I will work the counter until two a.m. Then Sissy and Jeanette will come down."

Molly was herded upstairs with the others. She saw Susana taking her shawl from its hook, Josiah putting on his jacket. They were leaving, even though there were stacks of dirty dishes, even though the stove, table, and floor had yet to be cleaned.

"You!" Gaston said to an assistant cook. "The mop!"

"Lazy greasers," Sissy muttered.

"They worked at least as hard as you did," Nell countered swiftly.

Annis stopped a quarrel from happening. "Good night," she told Sissy and Jeanette at their door. "I hope you can sleep. I hope we all can sleep." To Molly and Colleen she said, "You haven't experienced a holiday yet. Now it's time for the Painted Daisy."

"Those double doors won't stop swinging all night," Nell

predicted. "The whole town'll be on a shoot."

If a "shoot" meant whooping, hollering, gun shots, and the almost musical cascade of shattering glass, then Nell was right. Molly couldn't sleep. When Colleen suggested that they go sit with the others across the hall, she agreed. She accompanied Colleen to Nell and Annis's room, which, being on the train side of the building, was quieter. Violet and Iona were already there – Iona strumming the guitar, Violet giving her hair a hundred strokes with her hairbrush.

"No Midnight Express tonight," Nell regretted.

"I peeked downstairs," Violet said, through her hair. "The sheriff has already put his hat on the counter."

Annis answered the question on Colleen's face. "Every man who comes in will have to pay twice: once for his coffee and once for gas light repair. Tomorrow there won't be a single street lamp left in town."

"Will the men hurt each other?" Colleen worried.

"Some will," said Violet.

"I can assure you that the doctor won't be sleeping tonight, either," said Annis.

"Jeanette always works the early morning shift so that she can preach," Nell gossiped. "By the time she gets down there the men will be so boiled and blistered they'll be ready to hear about their sins."

"Sissy's hoping one of them will see her through his whiskey-red eyes and fall helplessly in love." Violet threw back her hair, clutched her heart and pretended to swoon.

"Your friends are surely home by now, Molly," Iona said softly. "It isn't safe for Mexicans to be out tonight."

→ ·⊰⧉⊱· ←

Susana and Josiah appeared healthy and sound the following morning. The counter regulars, in contrast, were a sorry lot. They hung over their coffee like sick dogs. Nell was censorious. "Too much of the oh-be-joyful last night. Chad Bellamy had better not show his face to me!"

Chad, wisely, stayed away. His friends, who didn't have as much to fear, begged for sympathy. Soffit began to shake his head at Molly's offer of a donut, stopped the movement, and groaned. Gravity sniffled miserably over his tea. Johnston mourned, "Lost my mule. Again."

"Headache powder," Nell snapped. Two words. "From Dacy." Two more. She slapped a small paper package on the counter. The men winced at the noise. Gravity, gingerly, unfolded the wrapping as if even a crackling sound was too much to bear.

"It isn't free," Nell told Molly, back at the coffee urn. "Compliments from Dacy today means higher charges tomorrow. They deserve it."

Nell was angry-irritable today. And so was Gaston. He blew around the kitchen like a snarling wind. "Too much salt! Not enough sugar! We prepare food! We do not cook *chow!*" He allowed no one to take a break, so Molly had to eat lunch by herself.

She went into the depot, where the postmaster handed over an envelope. He too, had a package of headache powder on his desk. "Another missive from your sweetheart," he said peevishly.

Molly opened the envelope as she left. *Dear Molly*. Her eyes jumped to the last line. A letter from Jonathan! She returned to the beginning and read swiftly. Too swiftly. The letter was very short. *Thank you for the poster. I am well. Ma is well. Pa is well. School is fine. Most sincerely, Jonathan.*

It wasn't a letter; it was a note! Molly wanted more. She wanted much more. She would have welcomed a Mr. Latterly style description of everything and anything. How many pupils were in their class this year? How many bushels of corn did Jonathan's Pa harvest? What would be the date of the annual sorghum festival? Jonathan should have sent *news*! By the time Molly got back to the counter, she was angry – irritable too.

But the next morning her mood shot upwards, because the postmaster handed her a package wrapped in so many layers of brown paper she couldn't at first feel the shape of a book. But a book it was, from Mr. Latterly. She and Susana sat on the porch steps, their shawl and sweater pulled close against the autumn chill, and they gloated.

"A gift for *Colleen*!" Susana congratulated herself.

The book opened at a bookmark, a tiny, blunt dagger with an elaborately scrolled and scalloped handle, engraved with the letters "CG."

"It's real silver!" Molly confirmed. "Two dollars, at least!"

The poem that the dagger marked was the only message they could find. "Read!" Susana demanded.

Molly tried. "*A Valediction: Forbidden Mourning*," she began. Like so much poetry of her acquaintance, the individual words she uttered made sense, but when put together they became a puzzling mish-mash. Some of the words she had never seen before. She stumbled over *inter-assured*. She pronounced *sublunary* syllable by syllable. When she looked up, she saw that Susana's expression mirrored her own lack of understanding.

"Who can tell us what it means?" Susana wondered.

The answer, of course, was twofold: Miss Lambert, because of her education, and Gravity, because he was so very cultured and British. Miss Lambert, now that she and Colleen were such good friends, would require too many lies. Gravity would be safer to consult.

"First," Susana planned, "you will hide the book behind the dishes ..." In only a minute, she had figured out an entire scheme.

So after lunch, Molly hid the book – minus the silver dagger – behind the counter saucers. She waited for Susana's signal.

"Coming!" Susana finally trilled, which meant that it was she, not Josiah or an assistant cook, who was delivering Jenkins' dinner to the counter shelf.

Molly immediately stationed herself in front of Gravity.

She whipped out Mr. Latterly's book. "What means?" she demanded loudly.

Nell looked over from her end of the counter, her eyebrows raised.

"Beg pardon?" asked Gravity, surprised. And then, observing the page opened to him, "Indeed!" Not reading from the page, speaking from memory, he intoned, "*As virtuous men pass mildly away ...*"

The other regulars stopped their bantering to listen. Molly could feel, even if she couldn't see, Susana beyond the green curtain, listening as well. Rendered in Gravity's accent, the words became smooth, beautiful, even glorious. "*... And makes me end where I begun.*" When he stopped, it was as if time had stopped. The counter was held in a moment of silence.

It was Molly who put them back on the clock. "What means?" she insisted. The cowboys returned to talking about cattle, the miners about coal.

"This," Gravity put his manicured finger on the page, "is the finest expression of love in the English language. It is a statement that when true lovers are parted, their love, instead of dissolving, stretches to greatness. John Donne. A master."

A great, "Oh," billowed the green curtain.

"Susana!" Gaston shouted.

That night, upstairs, Molly followed Susana's instructions exactly. She pretended to read, ostentatiously, in front of Colleen. Colleen, of course, made the obvious wrong assumption. "Jonathan sent you a *poetry book*?" Colleen frowned, as if trying to figure out the impossibility. Then her brow cleared. "His mother must have chosen it. It is a very proper gift." She flipped through the pages, not noticing that the book fell open of its own accord to where the paper was imprinted with the shape of a tiny dagger.

"Read that poem!" Molly insisted. "Imagine! What if it was written just for you?"

Colleen laughed, but she scanned the poem anyway.

"Do you understand it?" Molly was prepared to explain.

But, "It's marvelous," Colleen murmured. And her eyes followed the lines again, more slowly. She turned the page to read another poem, then another. She read until Molly could stay awake no longer, until Molly fell asleep. Molly slept with both a watch and a dagger beneath her pillow that night. The watch because it was her soul, and the dagger because it was the gift that would mark the day when Colleen opened to love.

→ ⚜ ←

Colleen may not have been in love with Mr. Latterly yet, but she loved his book. She read the poems silently and aloud. She read poetry in the evenings. She read poetry at night, during the Christmas holidays, while working the late shift with Molly.

Because Colleen was immersed in literature, Molly had nobody to converse with during that long, particularly lonely week. The men sitting across from her at the counter drowsed, awakened, and drowsed again. When Molly asked them questions, "Where from? How family? Miss home?" they always answered, but they often didn't have much to tell. They had become a forgotten people, possessing memories, but no longer having any real connections to their pasts. "My brother, Tom, now he was a spitfire!" one of the railroaders chuckled fondly. And then sighed, "Don't know, though, if Tom might still be alive."

Molly might have felt swallowed by her customers' loneliness if Susana hadn't invited her to a party. Susana and Josiah were taking a wagon full of Chihuahua children to the town of Cimarron, thirty-five miles away. They were going to the Saint James Hotel where Buffalo Bill held a big celebration every year. "That's where he started the Wild West Show," Susana explained. "You must come!"

Molly knew all about the Wild West Show. Jonathan had gone once, when the show was in Chicago. Jonathan had seen Indians climb up on each other's shoulders to ride in a pyramid on a horse's back; he had seen a cowboy lasso a real-live swan set aflight from a cage; he had seen a lady – a lady! – shoot a silver dollar tossed upward by some lucky attendee on the far side of the ring. The lady had shot that silver dollar dead center. Jonathan had seen the coin, held it, even. After hearing Jonathan's stories, Papa had promised to take Molly and Colleen to the show when Buffalo Bill next came to Illinois. But then Papa became ill.

"Buffalo Bill's riders, well, most of them," said Susana, "are men from Cimarron. Mexicans, Indians, Gringos. They return home for Christmas bringing their children the most wonderful gifts. And they always bring extras, for whoever else attends the party. That is us."

Molly couldn't wait to go. But she put off mentioning the plan to Colleen until deep into the night, when all of their customers had sunk into private dreams, when Colleen's eyes were soft with the cadence of rhyme. Colleen blinked at Molly's words. She shut the book over a finger so that she wouldn't lose her place. She gazed at Molly as if Molly were a character from one of her pages, something new, something unpredictable. "Yes," she said. "You've earned a treat." But then her expression shadowed. "Except that ... Let's ask Nell and find what she thinks."

Nell, when consulted the following afternoon, thought that going to Cimarron was a perfectly fine idea. "Have fun," she said. "And if anybody asks – anybody like Sissy! – I'll just say that it's very kind of Molly to offer to escort those children. I'll say that it's very Christian."

So on Christmas Eve morning, appropriately layered in skirt, shirtwaist, sweater and brand-new coat, Molly stood waiting on the Harvey House back porch. The coat was her early Christmas gift from Colleen. Colleen had ordered two from Mr. Dacy, one for each of them. Two very ugly brown coats, entirely in keeping with their Harvey Girl shoes. Molly pulled her red ribbon out over the collar. Mr. Latterly's golden four-leaf clover, once warm, turned ice cold. She bore her finger into the dented center, trying to wake up. She had only slept for two hours.

Josiah and Susana arrived in an old farm wagon with six small children bundled into the straw. The children all remembered Molly from the party in Chihuahua. Molly didn't remember a single one of them. "How do you do?" she inquired. The children giggled.

Susana jumped down to give Molly the warmest spot, the middle of the driver's seat. The children burrowed deep into their nests. "*¡Vamos!*" Josiah ordered the horses.

Molly was finally leaving Raton! It would have been a momentous occasion except that she was traveling west, not east. The wagon wheels shuddered into ruts perpendicular to First Street. The last vestiges of civilization – an irrigation ditch, a buck and pole fence – dropped away. The mountains across the valley were absolutely clear against the sky, some peaked with rocky spires, others looking as though they had been pounded flat by a giant's mallet. Close by, Molly mostly saw a sort of low, scrubby vegetation and a herd of deer-like animals that lifted their noses before speeding off.

"Antelope," said Josiah.

The antelope ran in rhythm, to a kind of beat. *Poetry*, Molly thought. And then she remembered. *Music!* This was the season for carols. She began to hum. A little voice, from the straw behind her, rose to fill the air like a treble flute. "Vitorio," Susana said softly. *Silent Night*. The words Vitorio sang were Spanish, but his tune, Molly's tune, were the same.

"When I was little," now Molly was dreaming out loud, just like her customers at the counter, "we would have a tree with candles and a star."

"There will be a tree with candles at the Saint James Hotel," Susana promised.

And there was, although the setting wasn't exactly homelike. The Saint James Hotel was really a saloon. Colleen would never have agreed to this outing if she had known. The saloon was something like a restaurant, but with a beautifully polished mahogany counter at one end. A huge mirror behind the counter reflected whiskey bottles, many sizes of glasses, a barman in a leather apron, drinking men at their tables … and the tree. A mountain fir, with packages at its base.

"There he is." Susana was so excited she grabbed Molly's hand. "Buffalo Bill!"

On the posters Molly had seen back in Illinois, Buffalo Bill had been huge and impressive. In person, he was shorter, older, plainer. But he had that recognizable jut of beard, he wore a handsome black suit, and his boots were as polished as the mahogany bar. He welcomed every individual child, whether Mexican or American. He shook hands with two black children and with a group of Indians. Perhaps they were Ute Indians, the tribe Miss Lambert had been writing about. Twenty-three children stared at Buffalo Bill's tree, so oddly decorated with tiny silver spurs and carved wooden horses.

With those children, Molly ate luncheon cheese sandwiches at the tables the drinking men had vacated. With them, her eyes jerked to the tree the moment Buffalo Bill drawled, "I don't suppose any of you believe in Santa Claus."

"We do!" they all, except Molly, shouted back.

"*Pleeeeeeeease!*" said Vitorio, and his one Spanish-accented word, made as long as a sentence, rose above the clamor.

"What?" Buffalo Bill put his hand to his ear, as if he hadn't quite heard. "Did I hear 'please?' Is somebody eager? Shall we start?"

"Yes," the children shouted.

Buffalo Bill handed out the gifts one by one. Each was wrapped in either muslin or calico. Just enough muslin for a shirt, wound around a pocket knife, for a boy. Just enough calico for a dress, tucked around a doll, for a girl. Susana pushed her Chihuahuans forward. Shyly, the children accepted. Eagerly, they unwrapped. "Thank you," they murmured, in passable English.

"And now for the smallest, we have something special," Buffalo Bill announced. The barman leaned down to where his mirror didn't reflect. He rolled out tricycles. Six shiny chrome tricycles, with purple plush seats.

Vitorio held his hands clasped as if in prayer. Buffalo Bill wheeled a tricycle his way. Vitorio ran, he leapt. "*¡Mira!*" he shouted. He worked the pedals. He crashed into a chair. Susana untangled him, and Buffalo Bill laughed.

"I also have something for the older young ladies and gentlemen," he said.

Molly stepped back. She had to. She was eighteen years old in New Mexico; she couldn't accept a gift meant for children. But she yearned. At that moment she would have given up her whole life for a surprise.

"So you'll always be pretty." Buffalo Bill presented Susana with a splendid comb and brush set.

"So you'll never be lost." He gave Josiah a compass.

"And you, my dear?" He was asking Molly's age, indirectly.

"I'm a Harvey Girl," she said sadly.

"Then you deserve something special." He reached into a pocket of his fine wool jacket and pulled out something small and shiny. He pressed it into Molly's hand. "So that you can call them to dinner, quiet them down, and herd them out the door." His gift was a whistle, heavy silver engraved with two intertwined *B*s.

Five dollars, at least. It was beautiful – much finer than Mr. Latterly's dagger.

All the way home, Molly blew her whistle. She blew it constantly, giddily. The trill was so loud, it made the children pop up out of the straw. It was so shrill, the old horses shook their manes and pulled harder. Molly blew at the trees, the mountains and the moon. She blew at the first lights of Raton. "Goodbye!" she said to her friends.

She jumped off the wagon, rushed through the kitchen and took a moment to stick her head through the green curtain. "I'm late! I'm sorry!" She darted upstairs, uniformed herself in a hurry, flew back downstairs, and carried out an order of a ham sandwich and two fried eggs.

Colleen wasn't overburdened. Only three men sat at the counter.

"Did you have a good time?" Colleen asked.

"Look what Buffalo Bill gave me!" The whistle was as bright as a star in Molly's palm.

Colleen touched it. "Bee, Bee," she said.

"It was his very own. Do you think he used it in his show? Josiah says it's loud enough to stop a train!"

Colleen laughed. "Go upstairs, sleep, and then come down early tomorrow morning when I'll be tired. I don't need you right now. I might go up myself when you come down, if it's still quiet."

Chapter 9

"Christmas bells will ring!" *The Atchison, Topeka and Santa Fe Railway Guidebook*

It was almost 4 a.m. by Papa's watch when Molly awoke. She crept down the hallway so as not to disturb the other girls. Colleen wore her late-night-early-morning look, a vacancy in her eyes that came from exhaustion. "Go on up," Molly urged. "I'll be fine." There were only three men at the counter. They may have been the same three men Molly had seen when she came home from Cimarron, but she wasn't sure.

Colleen refilled the coffee urn before she left. "More coffee?" Molly asked the men.

Only one answered, an engine wiper, still grease-smeared

from the roundhouse. "All right," he said.

But even as Molly poured, he returned to the nighttime stupor that he shared with the other two. They sat in a line, hunched over their cups, collapsed into dreams that would only deepen when the baker arrived. Then, drugged with the scent of rising rolls and bubbling pies, their sleep would become impenetrable. Not until the breakfast cook started frying bacon would they shake themselves back into consciousness.

Breakfast was an hour or more away.

"I saw Buffalo Bill at the Saint James Hotel yesterday!" Molly tried to awaken the wiper. "He gave me his whistle!" But the wiper, unimpressed by Buffalo Bill, the hotel, the whistle, or even by Molly breaking the no-more-than-three words rule, remained as somnolent as his companions.

Molly pushed aside the green curtain. The night cook was stretched out on the table, his eyes closed. Molly walked past him, sighing loudly. He didn't stir. She opened the ice box to pour herself a glass of milk, then shut the door firmly. He slept on.

Molly glanced at the clock. She only had five minutes to wait until the baker arrived, and when he did appear, his head and shoulders were white with snow. He smiled down at Molly's palm. "That's just fine!" he complimented. "Blow it," he jerked his head toward the night cook's table, "wake him up good." Snow flew from his hair. "It's coming down hard," he remarked.

Molly didn't blow. This was the whistle that could awaken a town. Instead, she stepped outside. The halos of light around the street lamps were a dizzy, spinning white. She put her hand beyond the shelter of the porch roof. In only a moment her palm filled with snowflakes – not the big, drifting kind that meant a short storm, soon melted. These snowflakes were small and icy, quick to stick and accumulate.

"Coming down hard," she informed the men at the counter. "Fresh donuts soon."

The wiper half-awakened again. "How much?" he asked.

"Of what?" Molly didn't understand.

"How much snow?" He had become fully alert.

"I don't know," Molly answered. "A foot, maybe."

The other men had woken from their stupors too. "That means two feet up at the pass." Now that his head was up, Molly could see who this second speaker was. Carson, one of the foremen from the roundhouse.

"More," said the third man who, during the day, knew a great deal about engine steam pressure. Carson had brought two of his crew to the counter to sleep off Christmas Eve. "Remember '84? The drifts?"

Molly remembered her one trip over Raton Pass. How high, how steep, how dark the tunnel. She tried to picture the pass in a blizzard. "Train due?" she asked. Two words.

"A special," Carson answered.

"Holiday-makers on their way to the Phoenix Resort," the wiper explained.

"What time is it?" the steam pressure expert asked.

All three men, and Molly, pulled out their watches. "4:30," Molly said.

"It's due here at 4:45," said Carson.

"They might have stayed in La Junta," the wiper hoped.

The steam pressure expert shook his head. "No reason to stay if it weren't snowing in Colorado."

"Then they stayed in Trinidad," the wiper found another reason to hope. "They had to stop anyway, to add on engines."

"Might not even been snowing then. Mountain storms can be sudden." The steam pressure expert was a pessimistic man.

Molly looked at her watch. "4:45," she announced, and they all listened for a whistle, a rumbling on the tracks outside.

"Only natural they'll be late," the wiper counseled.

"Trinidad will know." The steam pressure expert was out of his chair as he spoke, opening the night door. "Look at all this!" He disappeared into the whiteness.

Molly poured coffee for Carson, who didn't drink it, but instead put his hands over the top of the cup as if holding in the warmth, holding down his worry. Molly went into the kitchen to fetch donuts. The night cook was gone, and the breakfast cook had just arrived. "Well over a foot out there," he told the baker. It was 5:00 a.m.

"Miss Molly!" The steam pressure expert was calling her from the counter. Molly ran back. He had left the night door open so that some of the blizzard blew inside, snowing over the counter and the end-most swivel chair. "I need a pitcher of coffee, two cups, and how 'bout some of those donuts," he said rapidly. "I'm gonna sit at the telegraph machine with Talmadge," he told the others. And then to Molly, "Hurry, girl!"

It was a rude demand, the sort of tone no one ever used in the Harvey House. But Molly did as she was told. "What's wrong?" she asked Carson.

"Nobody answered in Trinidad," he said gloomily.

The telegraph lines over Raton Pass may have been silent, but there was an invisible, lineless connection amongst the railroaders of town. Jenkins, the freight agent, came in first, saying simply, "I heard."

Chad Bellamy showed up soon after, asking, "Any news?"

Molly was now pouring coffee for men she only knew by face and name. Dining room regulars, mostly. Few sat. Instead, they stood together in loose groups, moving from one cluster to another as if the news might change. But there was no news. There was no response from the telegraph office in Trinidad, and none from La Junta either.

"Isn't anybody awake anywhere?" a man groaned.

"It's Christmas," Molly said, but nobody was listening to her.

5:30. The area in front of the counter was crowded shoulder to shoulder, hat to hat. Molly wished for Colleen's help, but didn't have time to go upstairs. The baker and the breakfast cook, who could have been useful, weren't. They had joined the throng of customers, becoming two more pairs of shoulders in the worried crowd.

"What is it, Talmadge?" someone called. The night telegrapher pushed his way right up to the counter. He knelt on a swivel chair so that everybody could see and hear him.

"La Junta and Trinidad were celebrating last night. All night. The saloons just closed. The Trinidad telegrapher thinks the special went through. He's gonna have to wake somebody up, to be sure. He thinks two engines were added."

"Lord." A man's soft word, blasphemy or prayer, spoke for them all.

"I need you roundhouse boys." Carson held up his hand like a general summoning his troops. A third of the men followed him out of the Harvey House.

"What's going on?" Finally! It was Annis, with a sleepy Nell in tow. Molly was dripping the last cup of coffee from the urn.

"There's a train," Molly said. "It's late – too late. They think it might be stuck up at the pass."

"Go tell Miss Lambert." Annis was decisive.

"I can't …" Molly couldn't imagine knocking on Miss Lambert's private bedroom door.

"Do it." Annis and Nell took over the counter like the trained Harvey Girls they were.

Molly had to go upstairs. She had to lift her hand to Miss Lambert's door.

"What is it?" asked a sleepy voice.

"Miss Lambert, it's Molly. I'm sorry, but …"

"Come in," the voice sighed.

Miss Lambert in bed was almost as elegant as Miss Lambert in street clothes. She wore a pintucked, ruffled and beribboned nightdress. Papa had once sold a similar, but less impressive nightgown to the mayor's wife back home.

"There's a train," Molly said. "It's late."

"How late?"

Molly had to tell Miss Lambert everything: everything she'd heard, and everything she thought she'd understood. Miss Lambert understood a great deal more than Molly. She was out of bed immediately, opening a wardrobe twice as large as the one Molly shared with Colleen, selecting a plain wool dress, so much simpler and more practical than her usual garb. She changed her clothing behind a Japanese-painted screen. "Keep talking," she instructed Molly.

Molly talked. Miss Lambert owned a cuckoo clock even more intricately carved than Molly's old clock back home in Streator. The little wooden bird poked its beak past the tiny wooden door. "Cuckoo," the bird whispered.

"The train's over an hour late now," Molly finished.

"Go back to the counter," Miss Lambert said. "It's going to be a very long day."

Christmas day. It was both the longest day and the shortest day Molly had ever experienced. She, Nell and Annis divided the counter as they had done that first week of Molly's employment. The crowd had grown in Molly's brief absence. Johnston and the coal miners now mixed with conductors, switchmen and yardmen. The men wanted coffee, donuts, rolls – quick foods that they could hold in their hands while they paced and talked and worried.

Violet came downstairs dressed in her prettiest. She had begged this morning off to spend with her rancher. She turned her face, a question, to Annis. "Full House," Annis said, and Violet ran back upstairs.

Miss Lambert appeared. "Return to work," she ordered the errant cooks. "If one of you gentlemen would please check our boilers? We'll need plenty of hot water." Two men leapt into action.

Violet returned, uniformed. One by one, the other Harvey Girls reported for duty. Colleen, still blinking away sleep, Sissy, adjusting the hairpiece that increased her height by two inches.

Miss Lambert commanded. "Violet, bring the doctor." Violet disappeared.

"Sissy, we will need blankets."

Sissy sped away.

"Molly, you will keep the coffee urn full."

Since Molly had been doing that already, she had no place new to go. The urn emptied so rapidly, she was constantly running back and forth from the kitchen, carrying empty, then full pitchers. On one of her trips she saw Josiah shaking snow from his shoulders. Susana stepped around the railroaders tinkering with the boiler so that she could hang her damp shawl beside the stove.

"The snow is this high!" Susana put her hand at her knees.

The busy spot was more congested than ever, with Colleen carrying quilts, Sissy almost invisible behind her pile of blankets, Iona loaded with pillows. Molly held the dining room doors open to let them pass through. Railroad men were tugging the tables into a long buffet, setting chairs against the windows.

"Coffee, Molly!" Nell called.

Mr. Thomas arrived late, as snow-covered as Josiah. He came in through the night door, sliding on the now wet and slick floor. "Tell the boy to bring a mop," he ordered Molly. He asked Engineer Soffit, "Is there any idea as to when we might expect the train?" Which was the question everybody was asking, and nobody was answering.

Molly carried her pitcher back into the kitchen. "Josiah …" she began.

The back door crashed open. "Soup!" Gaston roared as he hurricaned inside. "You, baker, will stay. No going home. Bread. Many breads." His English disappeared into French. "*Mon chou*," he beckoned to Molly. She stepped into the still center of his energy. He took away her pitcher, handed her a knife, and pointed to a bushel of apples. He demonstrated with his hand. "*Coupe*," he commanded.

"Chop," Molly confirmed. "But I'm supposed to …"

"Molly!" That was Nell.

Molly tumbled some apples into her apron. She grabbed back her pitcher. "I can't *coupe*!" she told Gaston. "Josiah, Mr. Thomas wants you to mop the counter floor." She rushed back to the counter.

The townsmen were there now: Mr. Dacy, Sheriff Armbruster, Mr. Bloutcher, Attorney Gleason. And they all wanted coffee. Only the ranchers and cowboys were missing and they – "Two feet of snow and still coming," Violet said, when she returned with the doctor – were snowbound out in the country.

The doctor took one of Molly's apples. "Breakfast?" he asked hopefully.

"Harry will be out in all of this!" Violet fretted. "He'll be trying to find his cattle!"

"Violet, take a cake of soap and go help Iona in the lounge," Miss Lambert ordered.

"Any chance of some eggs?" the doctor pleaded.

"A message!" Mr. Thomas's voice was as loud as a gong. "Their baggage man cut into the telegraph wire up at the pass. He attached his emergency box. They're stuck on our side of the tunnel. Ten foot drifts."

"Saddle up your engines, boys. Break out the snowplows. My Little Buttercup will lead the way," Engineer Soffit shouted. And every engineer, fireman and brakeman left the

Harvey House.

The doctor got his eggs.

The rest of the day was a matter of preparing and waiting, in equal measure. The snow stopped, and the remaining citizens of Raton came to participate in the emergency. "You see, if he's got his portable telegraph box," rough and never-shaven Johnston explained to a cluster of fine and proper ladies, "and if he's near enough to a pole so's he can climb up to the wire, he can tap in and send out a message."

The ladies expressed their amazement.

Johnston expanded like a balloon at their attention. "It'll be a race. We can only hope our men get up there before the passengers freeze to death."

"Oh!" the ladies gasped.

One of the ladies stepped aside. "I'm Mrs. Maude Jenkins," she told Miss Lambert. "How may I help?"

"You could have blankets, quilts and towels sent from your home."

The day blurred for Molly. Somehow the whole town of Raton managed to fit into the Harvey House. The entire downstairs was a busy spot. Except for the kitchen. Gaston's roar was as effective as a guard dog at keeping out the Raton ladies. He and his workers spun through their tasks with absolute economy of movement and time. Gaston only paused in his efficiency when Susana's grandmother arrived with a group of eight Chihuahuans. Gaston bowed over the old woman's hand and boomed, "At last! People who know how to work!" He set one woman to chopping the apples. Other women dried dishes and scrubbed the table of spills.

"Molly!" Gaston caught her watching. "Bring Miss Lambert!"

Molly found Miss Lambert with Mr. Thomas, organizing a portion of the dining room into a makeshift hospital. "Some people from Chihuahua have come," she said. "Gaston is asking for you." Miss Lambert followed her right away.

"Gaston?" Miss Lambert inquired.

"These men," he responded.

"Ah! I have a job for them." And Miss Lambert turned to the Chihuahua men. "*Necesitamos camas*," she said. And then to Molly, "Don't look so shocked. You could speak Spanish too, if you tried. It's just another language. We'll need the mattresses from our rooms. Show these people the way."

Josiah detached himself from the sink where he was no longer needed. With Gaston's approval, he joined the men and followed Molly upstairs. "Four rooms?" he said, astonished. "For only eight of you? A room for boxes? And Miss Lambert has two rooms to herself?"

Molly didn't see Josiah in the kitchen again. For a while, she glimpsed him now and then through windows, shoveling snow off the depot platform. Then he disappeared, showing up later at the back door with Johnston and a huge load of coal. The Chihuahua men hefted coal to the kitchen stove. Josiah and Johnston trailed coal dust into the dining room. "Gotta keep this room warm," Johnston told his female audience, while Josiah shoveled coal into the dining room heating stove.

The Raton folk gathered around the warmth. They waited. The roundhouse men returned after sending off the locomotives. They waited too.

"You're doing a fine job, son," Molly heard Carson compliment Josiah.

Hours passed. Molly began carrying her pitchers of coffee directly into the dining room. She poured into the cups people held out. "Are you one of the two young women from Illinois?" Mrs. Dacy asked conversationally.

"Yes, Ma'am." Molly didn't have time to chat.

Finally, Mr. Thomas raised his voice. "Talmadge reports a message from the baggage man. Our snowplows are up there."

Everybody cheered.

But it wasn't until the street lamps were lit that Little Buttercup whistled her return. People surged from the stove to the dining room windows. They pushed behind Molly until her nose touched cold glass. Five monster engines rumbled by, and then Little Buttercup, her headlights burning, her bright yellow sides spattered with dirt up to Engineer Soffit's window. She pulled two passenger cars and a caboose.

"Frostbite." Molly didn't know who first said those words, but people ran outside. As each passenger or crewman disembarked, two or four Raton citizens escorted – sometimes carried – the snow victim into the Harvey House. Miss Lambert gave each newcomer a blanket. Mr. Thomas assessed their condition and told them to either sit or lie down in the dining room.

"We have warm baths for the babies in our lounge," said Violet, which was something Molly had been too busy to know about. Violet and Iona scooped up babies who were too cold to cry out at strange arms, and carried them away.

The doctor squatted over mattresses. He examined feet, fingers, noses. Susana's grandmother left the kitchen to squat beside him. The two shared no words. They seemed to speak through what their hands did for the patients. The old grandmother clucked over the heroic baggage man. She made him strip down to his long underwear, right in front of everybody. She wrapped every inch of his body in warm towels.

It was Molly's job, the kitchen's job, to warm people from the inside. Now Molly was pouring hot apple cider as well as coffee. Sissy heaved the kitchen's huge soup tureens out to the buffet. For someone so tiny, she could lift an extraordinary weight. "We're closing down the counter," said Annis, "as of now." She and Nell began serving from the buffet table. Colleen and Jeanette carried cups and bowls of soup to those passengers who couldn't, or wouldn't, leave the blanketed warmth of their chairs.

"I have sandwiches," Molly told Annis. Gaston was sending out more substantial food. The townspeople ate too, as much as the passengers. Still, Gaston provided. "Pineapple," Molly announced. This was a special treat, holiday fare. "Roast beef and crab salad." The buffet was turning into Christmas dinner. Molly was now bringing out platters of ham, turkey, asparagus, pickled onions, salted almonds, roasted buttered yams, winter squash, applesauce.

"We need more coffee," said Sissy. "I'll fetch it, Molly."

So many people, and yet the Harvey House provided. Colleen and Jeanette swirled through the crowd, carrying plates to the injured. Miss Lambert sent Molly back to the kitchen yet again. "The babies need milk," Molly shouted above Gaston's din. Susana grabbed her shawl and was gone.

Sometime during that long, long evening, a tree appeared in the dining room. Coal miners and railroaders and even some passengers carved trinkets for hanging. Molly walked around Mr. Bloutcher, who knelt before the baggage man. The baggage man now sat in a chair, dressed in different clothes than the ones in which he had arrived. Mr. Bloutcher was measuring the baggage man's feet. "Size ten," Mr. Bloutcher said. "I have a fine pair of boots ready-made. You just sit here and wait for me."

In the kitchen, Susana's grandmother and Gaston stood together at the stove, inhaling the steam over a pot that smelled of lemons and black leaf tea. Gaston uncorked a bottle of rum and poured it all in. "Grog," he informed Molly, "to prevent the cough, the flu."

When Molly carried the grog out to the buffet, the railroaders' heads swiveled like dogs at the scent. A darkly rouged woman in a bright red satin dress shoved the railroaders aside. "I'm Daisy," she introduced herself to Miss Lambert. "Let me pour."

"Thank you," Miss Lambert replied. "I do appreciate your assistance."

Daisy stationed herself behind the grog pot. "One cup each," she yelled. "And that's all! Passengers get served first. You boys stand back."

The railroaders and coal miners obediently made an aisle through which Colleen and Jeanette could carry their trays filled with medicinal cups.

What next? Molly wondered.

What next was Gaston. For hours he had been performing miracles. Now he left the kitchen as if on parade, wearing a clean hat and apron. The baker, breakfast cook, and two assistant day cooks walked ever-so-carefully behind him, carrying a huge tray. The tray bore a cake large enough for a wedding, but decorated for Christmas with garlands of bright red icing over white. The only way to achieve such red was by mixing in dried cocks' combs. "He must have used them all," Molly breathed.

Gaston's hat, his stance, his cake, silenced the crowd. Then Engineer Soffit began to clap, joined by the Raton residents and the people from the stranded train. Gaston didn't nod. He was too dignified to let his hat flop. But he did smile.

"You may cut," he told Miss Lambert.

Miss Lambert cut. The Harvey Girls served. Afterward, Molly yawned. Was it her yawn, or somebody else's that started an epidemic?

"Can you bear the snow again?" Mr. Bloutcher asked the baggage man.

"I think I can bed down your whole family," Mrs. Jenkins told a passenger.

"I can take seven," Mrs. Dacy volunteered.

The Harvey House emptied of citizens and passengers, leaving every single plate the House owned dirtied. Only the Chihuahuans remained, the women washing dishes, the men moving mattresses, tables and chairs. The Harvey girls cleaned the dining room, the counter area, the entry.

"It isn't even midnight," Violet said. "How could this day have been so huge?"

"All right, girls." Miss Lambert released her troops from duty. "That's enough. Go to bed. No night shift tonight."

Molly dragged herself upstairs with the rest. She made sure her window was securely closed against the cold. Surely nobody would be taking the Midnight Express.

"Sleep with this, Molly." Colleen handed her a hot water bottle. "Sleep well."

They settled into bed. "That old woman, the Mexican ..." Colleen said.

"Susana's grandmother," Molly supplied.

"The doctor trusted her completely," Colleen finished.

"He did." Molly was as proud as if Susana's grandmother were her own.

"Listen," said Colleen.

Molly couldn't help but listen. It was a cacophony of train whistles, all blowing at once, all coming from the roundhouse. "It must be midnight." But Molly was too tired to check the time against Papa's watch.

"They're saying good night. Merry Christmas," Colleen guessed.

"It was a Merry Christmas," Molly told her sister. "It was one of the best Christmases ever."

Chapter 10

"Skill, charm and beauty distinguish all the West's gentlemen — and gentlewomen — of audacious dishonesty." *Billy the Kid and Company*

Gaston had been magnificent on Christmas Day. But during the month of January, he proved himself to be a genius. Molly had never seen some of the foods he chose to prepare. Yardmen came to the kitchen door carrying washtubs filled with soft-shell crabs. Gaston examined the crabs one by one, talking to them softly in French.

"They are delicate creatures," he explained to Molly. "Ah! That they have survived the journey!"

"They were a mess of trouble," a yardman complained.

"Direct sunlight, they die. Train stops too suddenly, they die. A loud noise, they die."

"But they are perfect! Perfect!" Gaston cooed. And he began cooking for a season that Molly had never heard of before: Mardi Gras. "We must be fat before Lent!" he exulted.

For Gravity, and for those few dining room regulars he believed possessed *goût*, Gaston snipped off the faces of his little crab friends. Molly watched Gaston's scissoring hands, and her breakfast churned.

"Gifts," he scolded, "to us. No regrets. No funny feelings in stomach."

Molly tried.

"To be broiled." He dropped the crabs into a bowl of milk and pepper. He let them soak while he monitored the oven temperature. When the heat was exactly what he wished, he cooked them, briefly. Then he made Molly his taster. She put one of Gaston's gifts, one of his little friends, into her mouth. She closed her eyes. Just a bit of crunch, a fishy sweetness that spread over her tongue, an almost butter-like sensation going down her throat.

"It's wonderful!" she exclaimed.

And so the season continued. Turtle soup, a cress salad that Gaston said could only be seasoned with salt, pepper, and tarragon vinegar. A cake he called *Gateau de Roi*, which was kind of a pound cake and kind of a bread.

"King's Cake," Gravity translated, when Molly offered him a piece. "Usually served with champagne, not tea. Has the House any champagne?"

The House had.

Pineapple fritters in rum, cauliflower baked in cheese sauce, and a rice pudding that Gaston allowed Molly to prepare all by herself when she finally had a day off. She followed his recipe exactly. He hovered while she worked over boiling pot and ice-chilled bowl. "Slow stir on the rice," he advised. "Fast, fast, fast on the cream!"

Rice pudding day was a glorious day.

The following morning, Molly was back in uniform, her pocket, as usual, bulging with Papa's watch, Mr. Latterly's dagger and Buffalo Bill's whistle, each wrapped in its own handkerchief to keep it shiny and unscratched. On top of them all was a fourth handkerchief reserved for her nose. At the very bottom, where they absolutely could not jingle, she had tucked a handful of coins. Colleen had assigned her some shopping.

"Will you get me a packet of pins?" Nell asked, when it came time for Molly to take her break.

Molly darted through the kitchen, waving to her friends. Out in the street, it had begun to snow. She stopped for a moment to raise her face and put out her tongue. New Mexico snow tasted different from Illinois snow. New Mexico snow tingled, just faintly, of resin and pine. Molly was a girl with *goût*.

She pushed open the door of the mercantile, where most of her regulars were gathered around Mr. Dacy's cash register.

They had left the Harvey House just before the 8:43 dropped off its load of breakfast passengers. The 8:43 was long gone, but Gravity and gang were lingering.

"It you would be so kind as to order a nose ring," Gravity was saying to Mr. Dacy. "I will require the largest there is."

"For your own big snoot?" Johnston's witticism made the other men chortle.

"For my prize bull." Gravity was all dignity. "For the first Hereford in New Mexico. For the father of my new and excellent herd."

"If it gets here," Jenkins yawned.

"The last father of your not-yet-new and still-to-be-excellent herd was rustled off … where?" Attorney Gleason asked.

"Texas," Sheriff Armbruster supplied.

"Right now ain't the season for rustling," Johnston observed.

"Even Genius Jim hasn't been seen, hide nor hair, since last October," Sheriff Armbruster agreed.

Molly tuned out their banter. She selected black cloth for lengthening her Harvey Girl skirts. She picked up soap and Nell's pins. She moved through this store almost as easily as she had moved through Papa's. Just as Papa's store had been perfect for Streator, Mr. Dacy's goods exactly matched the needs of his clientele. She found a new hairbrush next to the shaving mugs. She carried her armload of goods up to the cash register where Johnston was standing, Gravity having relinquished the buying customer's position.

"You go next, Miss Molly." Johnston politely stood aside.

Molly paid, then couldn't help but linger, just for a minute, to see what Johnston would buy. She knew nothing about Johnston's home life. When she was little, she had sometimes guessed about people from the purchases they made. Now she tried to create a picture in her mind while Johnston listed: "Ten pounds of coffee beans, a one-hundred-pound sack of flour …"

The men in the store guessed before Molly did.

"Going out again, Johnston? In this weather? Not the best time of year to prospect," said Jenkins.

"… two pounds of salt, twenty of bacon …"

"He won back his mule last night," Attorney Gleason told the others. "I don't know what was wrong with me. I guess I just let him have all the good cards."

"… one of your cheaper coffee mills …"

"I got some lanterns in, Johnston," Mr. Dacy suggested. "You might need one for your dark, lonely nights."

"What's he do during his dark, lonely nights?" Sheriff Armbruster wondered.

"He dreams of lo-o-o-v-e," Jenkins guessed.

"… fifty pounds of beans, twenty pounds of dried beef …"

Molly had to be back at work. She left before Johnston finished. But when she was only halfway across the street, she heard him call her name. He had interrupted his purchasing to follow her. He kept her standing in the cold with the kind of idle conversation she had never known him to utter before.

"How are you, Miss Molly?" he asked. "Fine day, ain't it," even though the sky looked as though it could let down another blizzard any minute. "I expect everybody's busy at the Harvey House," which was a fact he knew as well as anybody else in town. "It was a real treat seeing Miss Annis at the counter yesterday, it being your day off. I mean, it's always a treat to see you too, Miss Molly. But Miss Annis … I've been meaning to ask you … Well, maybe you could tell me … I don't often see Miss Annis out at night, not like Miss Nell and Miss Violet …" He took a deep breath. "Does Miss Annis have a feller back home, like you?"

Molly could have dropped all her packages on the street and stepped on them, she was that amazed. Short, shabby Johnston interested in tall, always-neat Annis? Even on tiptoes he barely came up to Molly's nose. He wouldn't reach Annis's chin! But he looked so pleading, standing there like a dog kept out too long in the chill, that Molly couldn't laugh. She had to be kind. "No," she told him.

Johnston sighed out his relief. "Fine woman," he said. "I saw her move a table single-handed back there on Christmas, and I thought, she's a fine woman." He touched his hat and returned happily to the store.

"Oh, my!" Molly's exhalation fogged the air.

"Were you speaking to me, Miss Molly?" a cowboy politely asked in passing.

"No. Just good morning," Molly replied. She could have danced across the street, she was so full of laughter, except she had to be careful of the slick spots. She knew it was only right she tell Annis the news of her unlikely suitor first, but Annis was undoubtedly working in the dining room. Molly would tell Nell.

Opening the Harvey House door, she was as merry as she had made Johnston. The kitchen had slowed down after its breakfast efforts. Susana was adding flour to the bin at the baking center, Josiah was stacking dishes. Molly waved at them again before she rushed upstairs with her packages. She practically slid down the banister in her rush to tell Nell.

"What a corker!" Nell rejoiced.

Molly needed a bite of food. Just a bite. She had no time to sit with Susana. She carried a plate into the lounge. There she saw Violet, taking her break. There were Jeanette and Sissy, who had slept late and were only now starting their breakfasts.

"Guess what!" Molly began.

"I wouldn't want to." Sissy had long ago lost her Christmas congeniality.

But Violet played along, "What?"

"Johnston's in love with Annis!"

"That girl's got endless peach pies in her future!" Violet was as delighted as Nell had been.

Sissy wrinkled her face in disgust. "*I* wouldn't want him," she sniffed. "But I suppose he's the best *Annis* can do."

"Not that anyone has ever been so foolish as to glance *your* way," Violet snapped. And another Sissy-quarrel had begun.

"It won't come to anything." Molly tried to soothe the moment. "It's just a joke."

But Sissy turned her ire on Molly. "Engaged?" she sneered. "You? I can't imagine how you did it. Sometimes, Molly, I wonder if you lie."

Molly stood stock still.

It was Jeanette who saved her. Sissy's roommate and only-maybe friend. Jeanette, who was more apt to quote the Bible than voice any opinion of her own. But this time, Jeanette spoke as plainly, and as crossly, as anybody. "Oh, Sissy, for once, just for once, leave Molly alone. Leave everybody alone."

Sissy's hands lifted in a gesture of disbelief. "You! Even you!" As if she had been terribly betrayed.

"*Love thy neighbor as thyself.*" Jeanette was back to quoting.

Sissy ran from the lounge, leaving most of her breakfast untouched.

"*For where envying and strife is, there is confusion and every evil work,*" Jeanette pronounced. "*James 3:16.*" With a somber, steady hand, she cracked her egg with a spoon.

→ ⚜ ←

On Molly's next day off, Gaston selected her to be his proxy. A train from California had dropped off the weekly boxcar filled with produce. The boxcar would stay on the siding for only four hours before another train pulled it over the pass to the La Junta Harvey House kitchen. Gaston listed everything he wanted Molly to choose and bring back for him. "Avocados, broccoli, lettuce, spinach and carrots. You, little Molly, I will trust. You will pick out the best grapefruits, the best melons."

"May Susana come too?" Molly begged.

Gaston frowned, then laughed. "Go!" he said to Susana. "Help!"

Outside, the street was icy, muddy, slushy. As soon as the door shut behind them, Molly told Susana the latest Mr. Latterly news. "His leg is almost healed."

"Ah!" Susana was pleased. "Then it is time to prepare your sister for his coming. You must fill her thoughts with his praise. You must say his name whenever you can. You must link him to everything that is good in Colleen's life. Then, when she sees him, she will think that he is all she desires."

"Really?" said Molly. "I can do that?"

"Easily." Susana supplied an example, "*Mr. Latterly is as intelligent as* – no – *even more intelligent than Gravity.*"

"*Mr. Latterly is as handsome as* …" Molly began, but stopped. "He's not handsome at all." She nodded at a miner who was passing by. "But he's handsomer than Johnston!"

Susana snorted. "He is taller than Johnston."

"He's cleaner than Johnston!"

They giggled their way to the siding, where the doors of Gaston's produce car were already pushed open. Yardmen sat within, their legs dangling over the edge, tangerine juice dribbling from their chins.

Molly put her hands on her hips. She borrowed some of Miss Lambert's crisp formality. "You men must leave our produce alone."

"Awww, Miss Molly." But when Jenkins stepped out of his boxcar-turned-office, the men melted away like last week's snow. The yard carpenter was suddenly hammering again. An iron specialist leaned over to inspect a loose rail.

Jenkins picked up a bunch of dates from the ground and handed them to Molly. "I hope you find enough for Gaston," he said in wry apology. "When you're finished, the carpenter will drive you back to the Harvey House."

From behind Jenkins' back, the carpenter raised his hammer in impudent salute.

Molly and Susana got to work. They lifted and gently pressed. They picked and they chose. The best avocados, the greenest broccoli, the most tender lettuce.

Susana opened a flower crate. She removed a green stem topped by an orange, blue, and white blossom – a bird of paradise for the Harvey House tables. She stroked the petals as if making a wish. "Oh!" she said, with the sudden eagerness of a person who has just remembered good news. "Mr. Carson spoke so well of Josiah that Engineer Soffit has asked Josiah to become an assistant wiper on the Little Buttercup! Engineer Soffit says it doesn't matter to him that Josiah is an Indian."

"Really?" Molly hadn't even suspected. And secrets, other than her own, were difficult to keep in the Harvey House.

"In a few years, Josiah will become a fireman." Susana was

proud. "And afterward, an engineer."

Molly wanted to match her friend's enthusiasm, but for some reason she couldn't. The carpenter stuck his head into the boxcar. "Ready, Miss Molly?" he asked.

"Yes," she told him.

Back at the Harvey House, she was supposed to help with the unloading. But mostly she watched Josiah heft and carry boxes inside. What would it be like to no longer see his back as he leaned over the sink? Or his hand while he carefully copied words out of the dictionary? Or his expression when, after watering Gaston's rose, he leaned back so that his face could touch the New Mexico sky?

Fine food was the order of the day, dictated by Mr. Harvey himself, so Gaston could not enforce a Lenten fast. But he could, and did, explore austerity in the ingredients he chose from Ash Wednesday on. "From now until Easter, no crabs, no truffles," he declared. Now the Harvey House served only ordinary fare – veal cutlets from the Kansas train, parsnips mashed with potatoes and butter, apples stewed in maple syrup. The passengers still asked for second helpings, and thirds. They left clutching bunches of hot-house grapes in their hands.

"Persimmons from Oregon." Gaston considered that possibility. "Tart. We will bring out ..." and he tightened his face to imitate astringency. With Molly's help, he created a pudding that was tart, sweet, smooth, and absolutely delicious.

He repeated menus during this Lenten season, something Molly had never known him to do before. Every Thursday he prepared a fish stew so thick it could hold a spoon upright. Every Friday the Harvey House served mountain trout, pan-fried with almonds. Because Gaston repeated, because these recipes were so simple, because Molly could learn a whole dinner after cooking for only one meal, he didn't pull her away from the counter as often as before. "You know already," he said proudly.

Molly thought that she would mind. But she didn't, not terribly. She only had two friends in the kitchen now.

The weeks of March passed, then the first of April. One morning Molly stood on Front Street and felt wonderful. She twirled until her skirt belled around her ankles. She reached through the front of her coat, into her pocket, fumbled through handkerchiefs, and pulled out her whistle. She blew, exuberantly.

Annis was just emerging from Dacy's Mercantile. She dropped her package. "Molly!"

Molly calmed down, a little. "Susana and I have the day off together! We're going walking with Josiah!"

"Well, he certainly knows you're coming now," Annis said dryly.

Molly waited, with growing impatience, for Susana to arrive. Finally, she and Susana were promenading. They had arrived at the roundhouse. Molly was seeing Josiah for the first time in over a month. He had grown. Or maybe he was just standing taller. He still was much shorter than she was. But he was so confident, in such a new way, that Molly felt shy. Josiah had taken on the attributes of all locomotive engine wipers. No matter how much it was washed, his shirt would never be clean again. His fingernails were now permanently encircled with black.

"Mr. Carson says I must continue my studies with you, Molly," he said, in a new and deeper voice. "Mr. Carson says book learning will help me get on."

Molly was thrilled.

With engine wiper, Harvey Girl and kitchen girl dignity, they went walking. They strolled further along First Street, bypassing the freight yard. They left town for a country road occupied only by somebody's wandering chickens. The winter snow, long since melted, had become a thick and sucking mud. It built up on Molly's shoes. It approached her ankles. The occasional puddle spattered water to her knees.

"Mr. Latterly is always neat and tidy," Susana said ruefully, looking down at her own, increasingly caked feet.

"Mr. Latterly would be intelligent enough to stay off this road," Molly agreed.

"What?" Josiah was bewildered.

"Josiah, you are a disgrace," Susana said, instead of explaining.

Josiah looked pointedly at his sister's bedraggled skirt. He reached down, scooped up a handful of mud, and with one swift movement, swatted her.

"Josiah!" Susana yelped.

It was a chase game, Molly realized, that those two had played many times before. Josiah forgot his new, deep voice. "You can't catch me!"

"Help me, Molly!" Susana said, as she scooped up two handfuls of mud.

They were one boy against two girls, and Molly had the longest legs of all. She and Susana cornered, pounced, and captured. Susana sat on Josiah's chest to paint his forehead, nose and cheeks. Josiah rolled free and came up like a windmill, spinning mud from his hands onto Susana's face, Molly's face. Molly poured mud down Josiah's back. He retaliated by pulling the combs and pins out of her hair. Susana caught Josiah by the knees and he went down again.

"Stop!" Molly said. "Please!" She was laughing too hard to continue the war.

"Oh, my!" Susana released Josiah, honoring the truce. "Molly, your hair!"

Molly put her filthy hand to her filthy hair, and in trying to put it back up, made it even filthier.

"Well," Josiah remarked. "At least your coat was already brown."

"What Grandmother will say about you," Susana said to her brother, "I do not know!"

They could go no place but home, so they separated to return to their respective places of cleanliness. Molly's trek back to the Harvey House was peppered with comments.

"You look like you went splat!" said Daisy.

"Be sure to dry those shoes right away," Mr. Bloutcher directed.

"Fortunately, the Harvey House owns the very best of my washing tubs," Mr. Dacy laughed.

"I do hope Monsieur Gaston's hot water boiler is working properly," Gravity mused.

By the time she reached the Harvey House porch, Molly had heard enough. She debated. Should she try to sneak upstairs via the Midnight Express? But the Midnight Express was just that – an after-nightfall, secret route. It wouldn't be a secret anymore if Miss Lambert happened to see Molly climbing like a dark and dirty spider up to her room.

Molly put her hand to her hair again. She would have to tell everybody that she had indeed tripped and gone splat. She pulled together what was left of her dignity and walked inside.

For once, the greatest noise didn't come from the kitchen, but from the lounge. "He's a decent man!" Annis was shouting angrily.

Gaston hadn't yet arrived. The assistant cooks hardly noticed Molly. They were only pretending to work while they listened.

"So now he's back from *prospecting* with a whole pack of gold. Just in time to tell us that Genius Jim – who's been quiet for ever so long – robbed the Trinidad bank. Yesterday. What could be more obvious?" Sissy's voice was firm and sure and spiteful.

"What's obvious is that you are an evil-hearted girl, Sissy," Annis said back.

Sissy gasped, an inhalation that was almost a scream.

"You are, by far, the unkindest person I've ever known," Annis asserted.

Molly could have avoided the lounge door. She could have edged around the busy spot to go up the stairs. But instead, she peeked. She saw Sissy, Annis, Jeanette and Colleen, all on break. Sissy stood, the others sat.

Sissy sputtered. "How dare you!"

"We were hired by Mr. Harvey to be *women of good character*." Once again, Jeanette betrayed her roommate. This time she quoted from the recruitment advertisement that Colleen had clipped from the newspaper so long ago.

Sissy's cheek purpled. "Good character!" she raged. "Good character, indeed!" She whirled to make an exit and saw Molly. She stopped. Her angry sneer hardened into an odd combination of disgust and delight. "What about *her*?"

Annis's mouth quirked into a tiny smile of amusement, just as Daisy's had done.

Jeanette observed Molly solemnly.

But it was Colleen's expression that mattered the most to Molly. Colleen's face was a mirror, showing that Molly appeared even younger than she really was.

"Look at her. *Look at her*!" Sissy spun back around. She accused Colleen. "I don't believe it when you say your sister is engaged." She railed at Annis. "Just like I don't believe it when Violet talks about how Molly is a born teacher, or when Iona says Molly was meant to be a cook. Or when you," Sissy snarled at Jeanette, "say Molly has the makings of a missionary." Sissy backed away, toward Molly and the door. "I'm going upstairs. I have something to tell Miss Lambert."

When she brushed past Molly, dried mud fell from Molly's skirt. "Still making mud pies?" Sissy asked, with stinging sweetness. And then she was pounding up the stairs, down the hallway, toward Miss Lambert's rooms.

Annis watched the ceiling as Sissy's footsteps drummed above.

Jeanette put her hands to her mouth, as if to hold back words of evil.

Colleen dropped her head to the table.

Molly could do nothing. She couldn't reassure Colleen. She couldn't beg forgiveness. She had done the irredeemable. She had broken the most important promise she had ever made.

"*Mollllly*," Sissy called. "Miss Lambert would like to *seeeee* you."

Molly couldn't move.

"*Mollllly*."

Molly felt for Papa's watch. Handkerchiefs one and two, whistle and dagger. Handkerchief three, the round, flat comfort of ticking. She clutched the watch, she held onto Papa, as tightly as she could. *Tick*. One second. *Tick*. Two seconds. *Tick*. Three …

"Molly!" Sissy insisted.

Molly had to let go of Papa's watch. She pulled out handkerchief four to dab at her face. Her shoes left a trail up the stairway and down the hallway to Miss Lambert's office. The door was already open. Miss Lambert sat at her desk, wearing spectacles. For a moment, Molly's guilt and dread lifted. Spectacles were so ordinary, so very unexciting. Spectacles meant hope.

"Close the door, Molly," Miss Lambert instructed.

Molly shut the door against Sissy's gloating.

"Don't come in any further. Do you know how you look?"

"Yes." Once again, Molly's fingers sought Papa's watch.

Miss Lambert sighed. "Oh, Molly," she said. "I don't want to do this. But it's my job. Sissy has made an allegation. She says that you cannot be the age you claim, that you are not old enough to be a Harvey Girl." Miss Lambert removed her spectacles. Without them, her eyes were sad and weary. "Harvey Company regulations require me to investigate. And if it comes down to your word against Sissy's, I must send a telegraph to your hometown. So I have to ask, *how old are you?*"

The promise was now fully broken. Molly had to speak the truth. "Thirteen," she whispered.

Chapter 11

"Only the most fortunate traveler will ever view a Western mirage." *The Atchison, Topeka and Santa Fe Railway Guidebook*

Nobody was surprised. Everybody was very kind.

The 11:06 train arrived for an early dinner, but still, the other girls found free moments to come upstairs. Annis hauled buckets of water from the kitchen boiler up to the box room. She poured them into the hip bath all the girls used. "I told Gaston," she said. "And he was so angry at Sissy he made a mistake. He put cayenne instead of cinnamon into the chocolate cake."

Nell brought up towels warmed at the kitchen stove. She

knocked at the box room door, then stood with her arms held out and her face modestly averted from the sight of Molly in the bath. "There's just a little bit of cheese sauce on one towel," she said. "Be sure not to get it in your hair."

Dressed only in towels, Molly ran over the hallway's cold wooden floorboards to her room. She found clean underclothes and Mama's gray dress on her bed. Colleen had been upstairs. But Colleen hadn't been to see her. Not even to scold her in the bath. Was Colleen saying she couldn't bear to see Molly? That she never wanted to see Molly again?

Chilled by the possibility of yet another great loss in her life, Molly shivered as she dressed. With wet hair slapping against her spine, she ran back to the box room. She found Papa's watch, Buffalo Bill's whistle, and Mr. Latterly's bookmark still wrapped in their handkerchiefs, safe in her pocket. But she couldn't find her four-leaf clover of hope.

She dunked her arms into the hip bath and felt around. No ribbon, no brass. She knelt to run her hands over the floor. Nothing. She turned her coat, shirtwaist, skirt, and even shoes, upside down. She shook them, sending flakes and wedges of dried mud everywhere.

"We'll wash those, Molly." Violet and Iona were at the box room door. Violet dropped Molly's shirtwaist in the bath. "For soaking," she explained. "I'll bleach it later."

Iona examined Molly's coat. "I can brush this clean," she said. "I think. Maybe."

"Thank you," Molly tried to say. But she found speech

difficult. She had behaved so badly, all this kindness was impossible to accept. She sprinted down the hallway with her precious talismans in her fists. She curled up on her bed with Papa's watch sheltered at her middle, just as she had done that very first day as a Harvey Girl.

"Molly?" The voice at her door was Jeanette's. "I'm leaving my Bible here, so that you can take comfort in the words of the Lord." There was the thump of a book being set on the floor. "I think you've been very brave."

Brave! Molly hadn't been the least bit brave! Although, "I haven't done *everything* wrong, Papa," she told the watch. "I've been useful."

Colleen didn't come upstairs until after the 1:22 train left. Her entrance was heralded by the scent of honey chicken. When she opened the door, she was balancing a tray. "Gaston," she explained. She arranged the tray on Molly's bed. She pulled the chair over and sat down. "I don't blame you, Molly," she said. "Truly, I don't. I blame myself. I forced you to be something you aren't. I was wrong to bring you out West. I was desperate." Colleen's voice wavered. She bit her lip. "You did very well. You did well for as long as you could."

It was a reprieve at a time when Molly didn't deserve one. "What will we do now?" she croaked.

"I don't know." Colleen's hands worried her skirt. "I'll have to ask people for advice." She loosened her hands, a deliberate effort. "Try this," she offered Molly a dessert plate, dining room china. "Gaston baked it, just as an experiment.

He calls it *Gâteau Mexicain*."

Molly tried a tiny bite, just to please her sister. The sugary chocolate melted in Molly's mouth, thick and sweet and enduring. The hot spice made her damp eyes water even more. It was the strangest cake she had ever tasted, but wonderful too.

"The passengers loved it," now Colleen was also crying. "Gaston says, 'Sometimes the unlikeliest mixtures create marvels.' Well, he didn't say it exactly like that, but that's what he meant."

A knock at their door. Colleen wiped her eyes. "Come in," she hiccupped.

Miss Lambert no longer wore spectacles. "I am glad that you are here, Colleen," she said, "as what I must say concerns you, as well. Molly," and now she spoke directly to Molly, "Kansas City will send your replacement as soon as possible. I had hoped that you could continue to work for us until then. But no. Rules apply. You may, however," and now Miss Lambert included Colleen in her comments, "remain living in this room until your replacement arrives."

"Thank you." Colleen was grateful.

Miss Lambert didn't leave. Not right away. She paused with her hand on the doorknob to say, "You were not the first girl who lied to get Harvey employment, Molly. But I do think that you were the best."

The next morning, Molly slipped out of the Harvey House without anybody seeing her. This was an accomplishment of which she was almost proud. It took so much planning. She lay in bed until Colleen left for the dining room. She crept downstairs until she could just see over the banister. She waited until the busy spot at the bottom of the stairs was empty, until Susana, until every person in the kitchen, had their backs turned to her. Then she escaped with her shoes in her hand, her newly brushed coat over her arm, and yesterday's shame fully intact.

Unlike yesterday, she didn't step into First Street and begin greeting acquaintances. By now, she knew, the entire town would be aware of her predicament. Nell, with her two or three words, would have told the men at the counter. Armstrong had sent the message for Miss Lambert. The town's wireless, invisible telegraph must long ago have reached every shop, house, and ranch.

Molly circled Gaston's rose. She ran across the depot platform. She darted over rails into the wasteland that separated Raton from Chihuahua. Deep into this no-man's land that was neither American nor Mexican, there was a hermitage. Years ago, a railroader had towed in an old boxcar and made it his home. Molly climbed the crate he had left behind as a front step. She slid open the door. She saw an old chair, another crate that was almost a table, and a very small and aged stove. She tried out the chair. It was positioned so that the hermit could gaze out his door. Molly too, gazed.

The sun, low and southerly, slowly shifted until its searching beams hit her face. She didn't squint. She hardly even blinked. She grieved. "I could live here too." Her breath rose in frosty puffs. The temperature had plunged last night. Her words echoed in the shabby space. "I could take my meals at the counter, with Gravity and the others."

"You will need coal." Susana had found her. She stood on Molly's new doorstep. "Gaston sent me. Are you all right?"

"No," Molly replied.

"It must have been awful," Susana commiserated. "Was Miss Lambert frightening?"

"No," Molly had to say. "She was kind."

"Josiah found this on the road. I cleaned it." Susana tossed the brass four-leaf clover onto Molly's lap. "Mr. Latterly will come," she promised. "Colleen will fall in love. Your life will return to its old happiness."

Molly tried to smile.

"Until then, you will live with us. That is what Grandmother says." In the doorway, Susana was haloed by the sun. She made a dismissive gesture, including all of the hermit's meager home. "You do not need this lonely place."

Molly's eyes welled.

"Although I wish you did not want to leave at all." Susana glowed like an angel.

Molly dabbed at her face with her coat sleeve.

Susana glowed even brighter. Her halo was lit by a new and sudden spark. She blazed. The new spark began to smoke.

Molly sniffed the air. "What's that?" she wondered.

Susana glanced over her shoulder. "Somebody has set fire to a dead tree! Out on the southern line! It is a signal! Something is wrong!"

"Full House!" they both cried at the same moment.

Molly jumped out of the boxcar just as the roundhouse whistles blew. She and Susana charged to the Harvey House. First Street was filling with the men they knew as merchants and miners. Now those men carried rifles. Cowboys spilled out of the Painted Daisy to unhitch horses. Sheriff Armbruster was already astride. "Raton Vigilantes!" he raised his arm so that all would follow him.

Inside the Harvey House, Susana and Molly parted. Molly pushed aside the green curtain to see nobody – not a waitress, not a customer. She cleared away plates still warm with food. She cleared Gravity's steaming tea cup.

"Soup!" Gaston roared in the kitchen. "Much soup!"

Molly found Annis shoving a table, Nell lifting chairs in the dining room. Miss Lambert was directing. "Coffee, Molly," Miss Lambert said, as if Molly were still a Harvey Girl.

Molly filled a pitcher with coffee. She filled and poured, filled and poured. The big urn at the counter was still half-empty when she heard the rumble of a train.

"The express car is missing!" Mr. Thomas shouted, and the passengers were upon them.

Mr. Thomas sent the ambulatory passengers to Molly. They were nothing like the tired and hungry people she was accustomed to serving. These people were terrified. Some wept. Others sank to the floor as if their legs had lost all strength. A man grabbed the back of a chair. "This is for Mater," he said. "Excuse me, please, but this is for my mother." Mater hunched inside her furs, defenseless and old.

Nell and Annis rushed into place beside Molly. As a team of three, they served soup, rolls, coffee. They heard the same story over and over again. "Genius Jim." The name was a chorus behind every sentence spoken. "Somebody pulled the emergency cord." Genius Jim. "I saw horsemen riding toward us, the Gang of Brains!" Genius Jim. "They dynamited the mail car." "They blew up the express car." "They tore open all the baggage."

"Our train was carrying bullion." "Silver." "Paper notes — enough money to buy out the Chicago stock exchange."

"I was bringing home Japanese pearls for my stores," a man mourned.

"They broke into the safes." Mater's lips were moving. Molly leaned close, to hear. "My diamonds were in the mail safe."

"Two detectives died."

Molly worked hard to fill people's stomachs. That was all she could do. This wasn't like Christmas Day. These passengers wouldn't lose their fear over the space of an hour, assured that cold weather was safely outside and all danger in the past.

"I don't want to get back on that train," said a woman with broken feathers on her hat.

In the kitchen, Gaston was performing his usual miracles. This was not an occasion for a special cake, so he made a vanilla pudding instead, something that throats clogged by fear could easily swallow. Molly carried bowls to the people who sat on the floor. She carried one to the woman wearing the ruined hat. "But I have to get back on that train," the woman told her. "I want to be home!"

Over the passengers' clamor, Molly heard railway noises. Two Raton engines being linked onto what was left of the dynamited train. "We have to go, folks," the conductor was moving through the crowd. "There are new cars waiting for us in La Junta."

Mater's son helped Mater down from her chair. The old woman had consumed only pudding. "Thank you, dear," she said to Molly. Leaning heavily on her son's arm, she tottered off.

"Clean-up time," Annis announced. "And then more coffee, Molly. We'll have the Raton Vigilantes in here soon."

Molly carried dishes into the kitchen.

"Even the swiftest soup must be the best soup," Gaston was scolding his cooks.

Molly returned to the counter. But first, she pushed aside the swinging doors to poke her head into the dining room. She wanted, she *needed*, to see Colleen. Just for a moment. Just a glance.

And there was her sister, picking up a napkin from the floor, every inch of her safe and solid, secure from the evil that was Genius Jim. Colleen caught Molly's stare. Her lips moved in a silent, "Molly." She smiled.

That smile was enough. Molly could continue. She proceeded to the counter, but via the long way, past the big front door. Mr. Thomas was holding the door open while he and Miss Lambert looked out. Little Buttercup was building up steam. The cars behind had blackened sides and shattered glass. Little Buttercup pulled away, its rumble vibrating through the soles of Molly's Harvey Girl shoes.

"It's such vital work," Molly overheard Miss Lambert say to Mr. Thomas. "Serving food, serving courage. I'll miss it when I'm gone."

→ ⇜❊⇝ ←

No one knew what was keeping the Raton Vigilantes. Annis was slicing pies. Nell was wrapping sandwiches. "Miss Lambert is leaving!" Molly told them.

"Shh! It's a secret." Annis silenced her.

"It's a secret," Nell echoed.

Which meant that the Raton telegraph didn't have a line into Hermit's Meadow, and that Molly was the last person in town to hear. Annis gathered up sandwiches and pie. "I'll take them to Armstrong," she said, and left for the depot.

But when she got back, she had no news. "Nothing," she told Miss Lambert, Mr. Thomas, Nell, Molly, Colleen, Iona, Violet and Jeanette. She didn't speak to Sissy. Only Miss Lambert now spoke to Sissy. Sissy was being shunned.

"Did you know that Johnston's Christian name is Godfrey?" Sissy hissed furiously to Molly, when they happened to meet in the busy spot. "G. J.! Genius Jim!"

Molly fled to the counter.

"Ignore her," Annis said loftily. "I'm going to go help move tables."

"Sissy's not happy unless she's got our petticoats in a twist," Nell grumbled. "Let's grease the chairs, Molly," which was something counter girls only did during the slowest of shifts.

To fetch the grease, Molly had to wend her way through the kitchen. She found, then placed herself in front of, Gaston. She stood exactly as she was: Molly. Not an eighteen-year-old Harvey Girl. Not an engaged woman learning how to cook. Not an aspiring teacher. Just Molly.

"You!" Gaston waved her toward the table. A pile of almonds from California awaited, already blanched and peeled and ready for … "To cut," he instructed. "Like this." His left hand braced the nut. His right hand chopped with impossibly swift precision, cutting off a slice that was transparently thin.

"Oh!" Molly grinned. "I can't. Not right now." But she picked up the knife anyway. She balanced it in her hand before putting it back down. "Later," she promised, and she carried the pot of grease through the green curtain.

"At last!" Nell remarked, even though nothing at all was happening in any part of the restaurant.

Except for Mr. Thomas. Mr. Thomas paced. He made a continuous circle, from the counter, to the kitchen, to the dining room, to the entry, and back to the counter. Finally he announced, "Maybe I can learn something." The front door opened, then closed with a bang.

Molly and Nell worked on the chairs, dipping rags into the grease pot and rubbing goop around every moving part. Molly's fingers, like Josiah's, soon earned dark circles around the nails. Six chairs lost their squeaks. The seventh and the eighth began to swivel freely.

"Hello, there!" someone called from the entry.

Molly, Nell, all the dining room girls rushed to the entry to see … Johnston. But not the same Johnston they had always known – no, this man was a picture of successful prospecting, wearing all new clothing from hat to boots. "Mr. Thomas sent me." Johnston preened before the girls' widened eyes. "Borrowed my mule as a matter of fact." He smoothed down his jacket front. "They're bringing in five of that Gang of Brains."

"They caught them?" Iona breathed.

"They caught them!" Violet clapped her hands.

"Thieves shall not inherit the kingdom of God!" Jeanette joyfully intoned.

Johnston was almost tall in his pride.

"You were there?" Annis asked.

"Almost." Johnston's pride didn't diminish a bit. "Got there just when they were surrounding the last. Had two trussed up, one pulled off his horse, and another bleeding from his gut. Don't think none of ours was killed."

"Someone go tell Miss Lambert!" Annis said.

But nobody moved, because the front door opened again, this time for a stranger. A bespectacled gentleman who leaned on a cane with one hand while hefting a large sample case with the other.

Molly couldn't believe her eyes. Nondescript features, the mousiest of hair. "Mr. Latterly?"

He didn't greet her. Instead, his glance skipped from face to face above the black and white uniforms. "Colleen," he said abruptly. "We must go."

Colleen blinked.

"It's Mr. Latterly!" Molly encouraged her. "Mr. Latterly is here!"

"Our dining room is closed, sir." Annis stepped forward. "But we will be glad to serve you at the counter."

Mr. Latterly paid Annis as little attention as he did Molly. "Now." He beckoned Colleen with his chin.

"Coffee?" Annis offered. "A sandwich?"

"Quickly!" Mr. Latterly insisted.

His ardor was all wrong. He was, as Susana always said, an inept lover. Molly tried to help out. "You must give Colleen some time," she advised.

Mr. Latterly's speech immediately became more lover-like. "Circumstances have changed," he said. "*We must fly, into forever, with our hearts beating together*, as you once told me."

"What?" Colleen was incredulous.

"The man's pie-eyed," Nell diagnosed.

"Somebody tell Miss Lambert," Annis ordered.

"I'll go." Violet broke away from the entranced group. "Tell me everything I miss," she made Iona promise.

"Don't pack," Mr. Latterly was saying. "I'll buy whatever you need."

Johnston entered the conversation now. He had been scratching his beard for some minutes. "I know you, sir," he said, in a considering sort of way. "I think."

"I often eat in this Harvey House." Mr. Latterly was dismissive. "Colleen!"

"That might be," Johnston agreed. "But there was a passenger on that train. Tried to get off. Tried to get back on again. Then one of the Gang brought him a horse, and he rode away. You might could be him."

For an injured man, Mr. Latterly moved with amazing speed. With the crooked part of the cane, he caught Johnston's neck and pulled the grizzled prospector close. He dropped his sample case and put a tiny gun to Johnston's head. "I estimate we have one minute and forty-three seconds to get to our horses," he told Colleen. "Rush! Be as eager as your letters!"

"Letters!" And realization flooded Colleen's face. "Mr. Latterly is … Oh, Molly!"

Thought by thought, like messages on a telegraph machine, the truth was clicking through Molly's brain: Mr.

Latterly had returned; Mr. Latterly wasn't Mr. Latterly; Mr. Latterly was Genius Jim.

"You two join the others," Mr. Latterly commanded, as Miss Lambert arrived with Violet. "I want you all to surround me in a nice, tight circle. That's right. We're going to walk out of the Harvey House. Colleen, bring my case. Now, all of you, move!"

Molly moved with the rest, her arms pressed against Jeanette's and Iona's. They walked forward. Annis and Miss Lambert shuffled backward. Sissy and Violet moved like crabs. Colleen picked up Mr. Latterly's case and declared, "I'm not coming."

"Of course you are," said Mr. Latterly. "I didn't take this risk for nothing." And he quoted one of Susana's best lines, *"My heart will not be full again until it is filled with you."*

Molly was furious. She was terrified. How could she have been so totally, dangerously, *embarrassingly* deceived? She stuck her fingers into her pocket. If she only had something, anything, that might help. She touched the dagger bookmark. Too small. She touched the hard arch of Buffalo Bill's whistle. Perhaps. She rolled the whistle up into her fist, brought her fist to her mouth, and blew.

The sound, loud outside, was deafening within. Sissy and Violet screamed. Mr. Latterly's gun arm jerked away from Johnston's head. Annis seized the moment and launched, spread-eagling through the air, dropping all of her weight on Mr. Latterly's back, crashing him to the ground.

"What is this?" Gaston shouted, storming from the kitchen, followed by his crew.

Annis lay across Mr. Latterly's back. Miss Lambert stomped on Mr. Latterly's gun hand to free the derringer. Johnston sat on Mr. Latterly's head. Colleen promptly dropped Mr. Latterly's case to sit, hard, on the back of his knees. The secret side of the case burst open, spilling out small white bundles – handkerchiefs protecting pearl necklaces, diamond rings, a diamond necklace, a diamond brooch.

Johnston reached for one of the squares of white linen. He wiped his forehead. "GJ," he read aloud the monogram with obvious pride at his own literacy. "Miss Annis, you are one admirable woman."

Chapter 12

"The West is where the dangerously creative go to remake themselves." *Billy the Kid and Company*

"Move west, my friend, and grow up with the country!" *The Atchison, Topeka and Santa Fe Railway Guidebook*

The following morning, Molly took a stroll through the streets of Raton. She walked with a bouncing step, because she was a celebrity. Everybody she saw whistled at her, trying to imitate, but not even coming close to the loudness of Buffalo Bill's whistle. "Good for you, Molly!" they called. Just "Molly," not "Miss Molly." As if she were a young girl. Or a saloonkeeper like Daisy. "Miss" had fallen away from her life like the corset she no longer had to wear. It felt fine.

She strolled down First Street and up Clark Avenue to the sheriff's office. Today, it appeared, was a holiday for most of Raton. Twenty men or more lounged outside the sheriff's door. Johnston, in his new clothes, held court. "Not that I was scared," he was saying. He interrupted himself, "My, but don't you look like a basket of chips, young lady!"

Molly accepted the compliment with a grin.

"Have you come to see Genius Jim?" Chad Bellamy asked.

"I have," Molly answered.

Sheriff Armbruster himself escorted her through his noisy office to the surprisingly silent hallway beyond. The hallway air was thick with the odors of sweat, dust, whiskey, tobacco, saddle wax, and cattle. A half-dozen cowboys sat in a tight row on chairs borrowed from the Harvey House, guns in hand. "Morning," one whispered, as if not wanting to wake a baby. He moved his chair so Molly could see into the barred, windowless room that was the town's one jail cell.

Five of the dangerous captives sat against walls, their knees pulled up into narrow spaces so that they wouldn't disturb their slumbering leader. Genius Jim. Mr. Latterly. He lay on his back on the bare floor, totally relaxed. Only his injured leg was stiff. He looked peaceful, plain and insignificant.

Molly caught the glance of one of the Gang of Brains. Now *this* man was obviously a criminal. His mouth sneered; his eyes were greedy.

She studied Genius Jim again. This time she detected something false about the way he had adapted himself to the meager comforts of the jail, something too easy about his posture. Everything about him was a lie. How could she have ever thought he was a fitting husband for Colleen? She wouldn't even marry him off to Sissy now!

Genius Jim didn't move, he didn't even pretend to snore beneath her observation. He just lay there, like a snake ready to strike. Molly clicked her tongue with disgust and stalked away.

Clark Avenue still buzzed. "A whole army of federal, state and county marshals is coming to take them off to Santa Fe," somebody said.

"I'm going with them."

"Me too."

"It'll be the shortest trial in territorial history!"

"What about the reward?" someone asked. A vegetable farmer from far out of town. "I've heard there's a two thousand dollar reward."

Johnston actually blushed. His cheeks turned a bashful pink above his grizzled beard. "Miss Annis insisted I take half," he mumbled. "A remarkable woman! Not too interested in marriage, but says since I risked my life for the Harvey House, I deserve a share. As for the rest, let this young lady tell you."

"First Annis is going to have a proper bathroom built for the Harvey Girls," Molly informed the farmer. "She hasn't yet said what else. She's going to be the new matron. Miss

Lambert is leaving."

"Where to?" The farm must be *very* far away.

"She's renting that little house on Third Street."

"Miss Lambert needs some quiet time," Johnston amplified. "Seeing as how she's writing a book. I suppose she could've gone back home to Boston, but she says Raton's more fun."

Fun. That was not a word Molly would ever have used before to describe Miss Lambert. But sometimes it wasn't so obvious what a person truly was. Maybe Miss Lambert was indeed capable of having fun. This was a possibility that Molly pondered deeply after she said goodbye to her acquaintances. Miss Lambert's character was newly important to her, because that morning Miss Lambert had come to the Gerry sisters' room, to sit on their one chair.

It was Colleen who had done most of the talking. "I want to stay on here," she told Molly. "It's been a hard decision, because I know that you don't. I'll telegraph Amy's mother and ask if you might live with them. But there's another option, and I do hope you'll consider it. Constanza has kindly invited you to board with her. You could live nearby."

Constanza? Molly couldn't have been more astonished if the chair had begun to talk.

"I have been impressed by your diligence, Molly," Miss Lambert said. "By your openness to other cultures. By your quick and creative responses to adversity. I think we would get along well together."

The world was full of marvels.

"It's your choice," Colleen finished. "I know that I can no longer insist. Raton or Streator, Molly, which do you want?"

Amazingly, Molly couldn't say, not right then, not right there. And, even more astonishing, hours later she was *still* unsure. She seemed to be as unaware of her real desires as she had been of Mr. Latterly's honest – or Genius Jim's dishonest – intentions. Sometimes life was confusingly unclear.

"Blooming maggots!" It was a man yelling from the direction of the Painted Daisy. The sound was as unlikely as Miss Lambert having fun. Gravity's British-accented voice. "Catch the blasted creature!" A white-faced bull rushed down First Street, somehow loose from the holding pen at the freight yard. Shoppers leapt from the street to hug the sides of stores.

Molly reached into her pocket, pulled out her whistle, and blew.

The bull jumped sideways, changed direction, and pounded up Cook Avenue. "Get out of the way, girl!" Mr. Dacy shouted. Those few men who weren't up at the jail peeled away from buildings to give chase.

Molly climbed the depot steps as Josiah came charging down. "Mail for you, Molly!" he cried, and he flew to join the pursuers. The three old gents who normally spent their days on the train side of the depot, checking arrivals and departures against their watches, filled the doorway with their aged bulk.

"Gravity's prize Hereford," said one.

"Here it comes again," said another.

"Making a circle, it is," commented the third.

"Excuse me." Molly pushed her way through. The postmaster was gone from his window. Letters lay scattered on the depot floor, all of them addressed to roundhouse men. Josiah had been fetching the mail. Molly went into the office behind the window to find her own letter.

Dear Molly. It was from Amy! *I know it has been months since I've written.* Well, that was true. Molly could count on two fingers the number of letters Amy had sent so far, this being the second. *But I want to tell you some wonderful, exciting news! I hope you don't mind.* Why should Molly mind? *I've finally been kissed!* Molly did mind. She didn't like the idea of Amy being kissed before her. *Now here's the part that is a little difficult. It was Jonathan.* Molly's hand dropped as her mouth opened wide. Jonathan! How dare he! How dare she! Amy was her very best friend! Jonathan was her beau!

Or was he?

Truth to tell, Molly minded more about Amy's being first than about who Amy had kissed. It was a surprising thought, but Jonathan didn't interest Molly anymore. He was so – Molly searched for the right word, then found it – *young.* Jonathan's favorite book was *Billy the Kid and Company.*

She finished reading. Amy prattled on about her piano lessons, about the new kittens in the barn. Molly found her attention wandering before she got to the end. She was that bored. Her thoughts floated to the Harvey House where

Gaston was preparing *coq au vin* for dinner. The chickens were from local farms, but the wine came all the way from Burgundy, France.

Amy's letter stopped being a letter and became a fan. Molly waved air against her face. She blew clutter out of her mind. What remained were facts – and possibilities. If she stayed in Raton, she could become a kitchen helper, like Susana. Why hadn't she thought of that before? Gaston wasn't bound by the Harvey Girl rules. He could hire a thirteen-year-old. A thirteen-year-old who, when she turned eighteen, would ask to be promoted to assistant cook. And when Molly was very old, maybe thirty like Miss Lambert, she could be a chef.

She dropped Amy's letter on top of the roundhouse mail. She darted out of the depot door – the old gents were gone now – and onto the street. She almost collided with Josiah.

"Whoa!" he said. "No need. They caught it. They are putting the bull back in the pen."

Molly halted, but only for a second. Time was marching on, just as the engraving said on Papa's watch. Molly was speeding into her future. She looked down at Josiah – she was probably four inches taller than he. She would have to bend over when she got around to kissing him. But right now, there was Miss Lambert on the Harvey House porch, actually laughing, laughing with Gravity. And Gaston inside the kitchen, expecting Molly's help. And Colleen, all alone in the dining room, waiting for Molly to decide.

As if Molly would ever leave her sister. Who could even

think such a thing? It was inconceivable! Colleen needed Molly. Colleen could never manage without her. Their times were meant to march on together. They were family, after all.

AUTHOR'S NOTE

When my great-grandmother, Jennie, was 22 years old and living in Streator, Illinois, she answered one of those Harvey ads for *young women of good character*. She left her family and friends to take an Atchison, Topeka and Santa Fe train out to the Wild West. The year was 1887.

I wish I knew more about Jennie's days as a Harvey Girl in the Raton Harvey House. Unfortunately, she left no letters or diaries for her great-grandchildren to read. Instead, she left things: I have her painted fan, mended silk stockings, and a gorgeous green dress with a high collar and whaleboned bodice.

And I have her gold watch, inscribed, *From George to Jennie, Christmas 1889.* (George was the brakeman-promoted-to-conductor who became my great-grandfather.) That watch sits on my desk now, as it has during the writing of *When Molly Was a Harvey Girl*.

Much of what is in this book is true. Much isn't. That's the nature of fiction. You put together imaginary characters with a library's worth of research, and you have a story. I often start with an idea, but this time I started with an inspiration: I opened the door into my own family's past.

P.S. If you'd like to know more about the Harvey Girls, look for:

The Harvey Girls: The Women Who Civilized the West by Juddi Morris

The Harvey Girls: Women Who Opened the West by Lesley Poling-Kempes

"The Harvey Girls" – a movie starring Judy Garland and based upon a 1942 novel, *The Harvey Girls* by Samuel Hopkins Adams

If you'd like to know more about desperados:

The Authentic Life of Billy the Kid: the Noted Desperado of the Southwest, Whose Deeds of Daring and Blood Made His Name a Terror in New Mexico, Arizona and Northern Mexico by Pat F. Garrett

Robbers, Rogues, and Ruffians: True Tales of the Wild West by Howard Bryan

And this was my very favorite reference, published in 1890 and now available online from openlibrary.org:

Rand McNally & Co.'s New Guide to the Pacific Coast.

Santa Fé Route: California, Arizona, New Mexico, Colorado and Kansas by James W. Steele

Jennie in 1885

George in 1891

The staff of the Raton Harvey House in 1894

Courtesy of the Arthur Johnson Memorial Library, Raton, New Mexico